LOVES, LIVES, AND LATTES

~ This is a lighthearted tale of how
local handyman Jimmy and his friends
deal with life, death, nosy neighbors,
and love. ~

DAVID LASTINGER

Loves, Lives, and Lattes

Copyright © 2024 by David Lastinger

All rights reserved.

ISBN: 978-1-7368578-2-3

This book is a work of fiction. Names, characters, business, events, and incidents are the products of the author's imagination. Any resemblance to actual persons, living or dead, or actual events is purely coincidental.

Cover creation by Ravi Verma from rdezines

Developmental editing by Emma O'Connell

Line editing and formatting by Lorraine Reguly from https://WordingWell.com

Dedication

This book is dedicated to my Godmother, Aunt Peggy. Without her gentle southern pushing and constant cheerleading, this book never would have happened.

Table of Contents

Chapter 1: How it All Started

It was a sunny Saturday morning at the end of spring. Jimmy and Papa Joe Harper were at their favorite table at The Coffee Stand, a neighborhood gathering place that had been around for the last 30 years, since 1977. Although it was now 2007, it was still owned by the same family. The place was buzzing with customers coming in for their share of fresh coffee and buttery croissants.

The university rejection letters lay on the table in front of them, torn in pieces. After the last six months, this was not the answer they were looking for.

"Well, son, what do you think you will do now?" asked Papa Joe.

Jimmy was tall for a young man, and had bushy blond hair that never looked tidy, no matter what he did to it.

"Damned if I know, Dad. I was just happy to finish the semester and graduate. It was really Mom's idea for me to go to college and have a career. Now that she is gone…" Jimmy's voice trailed off, remembering how he found her. Right in the middle of his senior year in high school, Emma, his mom, died from a brain aneurism that no one saw coming. Jimmy found her lifeless body on the living room floor.

A server stopped by the table to refill their coffee cups. After she walked away, Papa Joe took a sip from his freshly filled cup and responded, "Yeah, I know she did, Jimmy. She really wanted to see you in college, and have a promising career, maybe even a wife."

Papa Joe's hair was cut short, in the same style he had in the Navy, just a little more salt and pepper now. With a twinkle in his eye, it seemed he was always ready with a joke and a smile.

"I know, Dad. I have no idea how I'm going to keep all those promises I made to her."

Jimmy's eyes almost teared up again. This was the third rejection letter he had received and he was beginning to lose hope. The letters were vague as to why he was being rejected but it was probably due to his last semester of low grades and his lack of attendance. But after losing his mom so suddenly, he just couldn't focus in school. He was grieving too badly.

He bit into a flaky croissant, evidenced by the flakes that fell all over his shirt. He brushed them off.

Just then, the door to the coffee shop jingled as it opened. A tall red-headed teenage girl walked in with someone who was probably her dad. Papa Joe looked at Jimmy and smiled.

"Well, son, the college thing might not be working out, but what do you think about her for a wife?" Papa Joe nudged his head in the pretty young woman's direction.

Jimmy scoffed at the idea. "Yeah, right, Dad. There's no way she would be attracted to me."

Papa Joe laughed and then sighed. The two newest customers headed toward the patio.

"Getting back to the subject at hand, I am still figuring stuff out, too. I hadn't realized how much I had counted on her 'til now. I can only hope that I was enough for her, too.

"Tell you what, we can take the whole summer to figure out what you want to do, but I will need you to find a job of some sort. I can't cover everything on my Navy retirement. Her work's life insurance just barely covered her funeral costs." Joe Harper always had a good bond with his son. He was a kid's kinda dad and Jimmy's friends liked him. He could fix anything, make everyone laugh, and even though he was permanently in a wheelchair, he could still flip a pancake onto a plate from across the room. Jimmy's mom was quieter than Papa Joe and had a wicked sense of humor. Most likely, that's where Jimmy got his sense of humor from. Emma was also very practical about life, and Jimmy always knew that he could talk to her about anything. Every once in a while, she would show off her silly side. He was going to miss that the most.

"Yeah, Dad, that's okay by me. Mom sure would have been good to talk to about all this. I had only one visit with the school career counselor. He wasn't much help and was a dingbat anyway. I have some friends who work in restaurants and bars around town. Maybe I will ask them. But I also hear horrible customer service stories from them, so, we'll see what happens."

"Speaking of your buddies, what are they going to do this summer? I'm sure you'd like to hang out with them as much as possible before *they* head off to college or wherever they are going."

"Calvin is going to be a teacher. Both of his parents are teachers, and one of his uncles is, as well. It seems to run in their family. He got accepted into Teacher's College."

Papa Joe nodded. "He's a smart one. I think he will do well. What about the other guy, Alex?"

Jimmy started laughing. "Oh, man, Dad. I love that guy, but he can't seem to stay out of trouble! He's in jail right now for auto theft. His family needed the money and it was quick cash for him. His family is not doing well since his dad ran out and left him with just his mom. He's smart but can't resist the adrenaline rush and cash that comes with it."

Papa Joe shook his head. "Hmm. I like him, too. He is always respectful. I hope he figures it out before it's too late."

Papa Joe looked thoughtful for a moment.

"You know, Jimmy, you are pretty handy with tools. I was thinking about this the other day. What if I put out the word to your mom's friends that you can take on some handyman jobs while we are looking for a job for you? It would certainly help in the cash department."

Jimmy took a long sip of his coffee. He liked the way it warmed the back of his throat.

"Yeah, I suppose that would be okay. It's kinda fun fixing stuff. I'd like that."

Jimmy had started feeling the weight of making real-life decisions, and it was a feeling he wasn't quite used to yet. He had never really considered a hands-on job before, as many of his school friends were considering jobs in medicine or business. The more he thought about it, the more he liked it.

Papa Joe leaned forward in his chair. In a lower voice, he confided, "Ya know, Jimmy, before I landed in this wheelchair, I made a living with my hands, too. Even my dad said as long as I could work with my hands, I could always find a job somewhere."

* * * * *

Meanwhile, Lauren Perry, the pretty redhead that had caught Jimmy's eye, was having a similar discussion with her dad, Finn, while they had lattes on the shaded patio. Unfortunately, Lauren's mood wasn't exactly as cool.

"Dammit, Dad, We've talked about this already! Why do you keep needling me about it?"

Her coffee cup clanged on the metal table as she firmly put it down. Lauren's dad put his cup on the table just as loudly, causing the patrons around them to turn their heads toward the daughter-father duo.

"I just don't understand why you have to go out of state. Is my alma mater not good enough for you? It's always been a top school in the country." He lowered his voice as he realized that it had gotten a little louder. "It was good enough for me."

Of course, her dad wanted his little girl to stay in the state. It just wasn't his choice anymore. He was an amazing dad. He never made her feel like she missed out on growing up without a mom, but she was *so* ready to get out in the world and see what it had to offer. Lauren needed him to be okay with that.

"Look, Dad, there is nothing wrong with your school. I'm eighteen now and you have been preparing me to leave the nest all my life. Now you have a change of heart? Bullshit! What are you really afraid of, Dad?"

Finn sat back in his chair with a long sigh. Then he leaned forward again.

"You're gonna make me say it. Well, *fine*. I am going to miss you more than you know. With you and your friends here all the time, the house was alive."

"Dad, no one but you could love me like you do, and I owe all of this to you."

She put her fingers and thumbs together in the shape of a halo over her head and batted her eyes at him.

The memory brought a smile to the old man's face.

"Damn it, Lauren! How do you always know how to make me giggle and lose an argument? Come here." He stood up and opened his arms. She stood up, too, and ran around the table to hug her dad. She was going to miss him.

"Dad, you know in your heart that the school in Washington has a better program than yours does. They're also giving me a full ride. Your school didn't offer me that, even though it's in-state. I can't exactly say 'No' to four years of free tuition!"

His face got serious again for a minute. "Yeah, I'm still kinda mad that they didn't!"

"Dad, I'm going to be just fine. I'm going to be in one of the best Interior Design programs there is!"

"Oh, sweetie, I know you will be. I just had to try one more time before you're all grown up and stuff."

Lauren sat back in her chair with a grin on her face, happy that she had won the argument. The smile didn't last long. She cocked her head slightly to the side and realized that she would soon leave the comfort and welcome feeling of her home—and favorite coffee shop—for the unknown. She leaned forward and rested her elbow on the table, cupping her chin in her hand. She noticed her dad's eyes were misty.

With a sniff, he wiped his eyes on his shirt.

"Let's settle our bill. We have a tee time in about an hour."

* * * * *

Later that morning, after returning from coffee and running a few errands, Jimmy went to his room.

From under the bed, he pulled out the leather journal he had gotten for Christmas and began writing.

Dear Mom,

12

I guess you already know about the rejection letters. I know I made all those promises to you about life, but I was planning to have those with you by my side. I don't know how I am going to do that now. I miss you so much.

Dad brought up the idea of being a handyman. I hadn't really figured on a non-college career, but the idea is starting to grow on me. Helping Dad out with the expenses only seems like the right thing to do, and I am okay with that. I'll let you know what happens.

Chapter 2: Old School, New School

A few days later, Jimmy knocked on Mrs. Otterminder's door. She was an old friend of his mom's.

"Hi, Jimmy. Thanks for coming over." She opened the door and greeted him with a big smile on her face. Placing her hands on her hips, she gushed, "Oh, Jimmy, I remember when you were just a little thing. You still have the same curly blond hair. It's nice to see you all grown up and handsome."

Jimmy turned red and tried to change the subject.

"Aww, thanks. Dad said you have some things around the house that need tending to."

Mrs. Otterminder continued on, not taking the hint. "Oh, Jimmy, I miss your mom. We were on the same nursing team at the Veterans Hospital where she met your dad. Everyone knew it was love at first sight. I bet you miss her, too."

"Yeah, I do. It's been a little quiet in the house, but we are getting it figured out." Jimmy rubbed his hand together as if to warm them up. "So, what needs fixing?"

"Oh, right, of course," she said with a giggle. "Well, the disposal is jammed and there are a few light bulbs that I can't reach. I am scared to climb a ladder at my age. "

Jimmy nodded in agreement.

"I totally get that. I'll get started and holler at you when I'm done."

Mrs. Otterminder still worked the occasional shift at the hospital, but she wasn't working today.

The tasks were simple and he had them completed with no trouble within an hour.

He even fixed a few things that weren't on her list but should have been.

"Hi, I am all done. Everything is good to go now. I just want to remind you that potato peels and coffee grounds cannot go down the disposal."

"Oh, Jimmy, you have made an old lady happy. I will try to remember that. How much do I owe you?"

"I have no idea. I've never charged for helping out, so whatever you want to give will be okay with me."

She had a big smile on her face as she reached for her purse. She handed him some folded-up bills.

He pocketed them right away and turned toward the front door.

"By the way, Jimmy, do you have a girlfriend yet?"

Jimmy shook his head to indicate "no" as he smiled at her.

"Well, that's a pity. One day you are gonna make some lucky girl a fine husband."

"Thanks, Mrs. Otterminder. I am not in a hurry. Whenever it happens, it will happen. See ya later."

As Jimmy drove away from her house, he couldn't help thinking about how nice it felt to help someone who needed his services. No matter how easy the task seemed to him, it was a big deal for his customer. He started to feel a sense of pride and satisfaction in the work. Like his dad said, "The money will come."

* * * * *

Word got around the neighborhood that summer that Jimmy Harper was doing handyman work. Within the month, he had already been to ten different houses. He was amazed that people were calling him for help.

After dinner one Saturday night, Jimmy cracked open a beer each for him and Papa Joe as they sat on the front porch. It was something they liked to do after dinner.

"Well, Jimmy, it looks like you have been quite popular with the old ladies," Joe ribbed his son, laughing.

"I know, right? It feels really nice to help them. The cash doesn't hurt either."

"Ya know, son, that could be a nice respectable business you have going there. People seem to like you and your work and they are happy to pay you for it. Low overhead too. You don't even need a shop."

Jimmy took a long pull on his beer.

"That thought occurred to me, too. I think I will do this through the rest of the summer and see how it goes. At least I won't be sitting at a desk or crazy hours at a restaurant."

* * * * *

With this part of Jimmy's future on the right track, he began to think about one of the other promises that he had made to his mom: finding a nice girl to marry someday. This part worried him more because he had tried dating in the past and it didn't work out very well.

For some reason he didn't know, he always got turned down.

That got him interested in using one of the popular dating apps. How hard could it be? Just put your profile in and wait for something to pop up. It seemed a lot easier than walking up to a girl in a grocery store or mall and asking her out. He had done that a few times and was shot down every time. Unfortunately, the app didn't work out as well as he'd hoped.

He had been chatting with Ashley, his first match, for a few weeks. She was smart and fun to chat with.

Jimmy was feeling pretty good about this. He opened a new chat and sent a text to her.

'Hey, it seems like we are chatting pretty well. Should we meet in person? Maybe do lunch?'

He had drummed out of the longest three songs ever from the radio on his steering wheel before his phone lit up again.

'Yeah, that sounds good. How about this Friday at noon at Clancy's Pub?'

'Great, I will see you there. I can't wait.'

* * * * *

Clancy's was busy that day at lunchtime. The only table available was a table for three.

Already nervous about meeting her, Jimmy got there early and waited for her to arrive. He recognized her immediately as he saw her brown curly hair bounce through the doorway. She was wearing the blue sundress that she said she would and gave Jimmy a big hug as he stood to greet her.

"You must be Ashley," he said with a smile. He thought she looked even better in person.

"Well, of course, I am. Unless you just hug every cute girl that walks in the door." Ashley smiled and winked at him.

"Shoot, I wish I were that lucky," he said shyly.

They took their seats. They had just finished ordering when another young lady walked up to their table. Jimmy looked puzzled as she approached.

"Ashley, is that you?" she said excitedly.

"Oh, my God, Lisa! How are you? What are you doing here? Funny running into you here!"

"I was coming in for lunch and saw you across the bar. It's crazy busy, and it looks like I may not get a table." Ashley reached up and gave a big hug to Lisa. Then she pointed to the third chair and motioned for her to have a seat.

"Nonsense, this one is free. Just join us, it's only a lunch date. Jimmy, this is my bestie, Lisa. You won't mind, will you?"

It didn't really sit well with him, but it was his first date, and a date is a date, so he figured he would at least try to see it through.

"Oh, sure, by all means, have a seat." He forced a smile. *Is this how dating is done now? Maybe I am too old for this stuff now.*

Lisa turned to Jimmy, "So, how do you know Ashley?"

"Well…" He paused. "Not very well yet, this is our first date." He raised his eyebrows at her, trying gently get her to leave them on their own.

"Aw, how sweet. How's it going so far?"

"Umm, it's been unique… so far," Jimmy answered with a slight rise in his voice.

Ashley leaned over to Lisa, "See, I told you he was a nice guy." She lowered her voice. "Order what you want. He's paying."

It wasn't quiet enough. Jimmy heard what she said. The smile faded from Jimmy's face.

He spoke up. "Ashley, I am a little confused. It seems like you brought a friend along on our first date?"

As nonchalant as ever, "Oh, I do it with all my first dates. A girl can't be too careful, ya know."

19

"Oh, so this wasn't a fun coincidence? Has that been working for you? The other guys didn't object?"

Lisa was beginning to look uneasy as the tension grew at the table.

"They didn't object at the time, so I figured it was okay," she said with a smile, still trying to play it down.

"I would imagine our food will be here soon. I'm going to go to the bathroom and will be right back. Start without me, for sure."

Jimmy stood up and excused himself from the table.

He walked down the hallway. Once he was out of their sight, he approached a man wearing a tie who seemed to be in charge.

"Hi, are you the manager?" Jimmy asked.

"I am. John Clancy is my name and this is my place. How can I help you?"

Jimmy discreetly pointed to his table and the two girls. The food had arrived by then and they were laughing and having a good chat.

"Do you see the blonde and brunette over there? The brunette and I were on a first date and the blonde 'accidently, on purpose' showed up. Apparently, they had planned it that way. Anyway, that's not my style."

John shook his head and sighed.

"I agree with you, sir. That ain't right."

"Here's some cash to cover the bill, but I don't wanna stick around to see how this turns out."

"Ahh, you are a good man. Don't worry about this. I will take care of it for you. Here's my card. I hope that you come back soon. When you do, the first round is on me."

They shook hands and Jimmy scooted out a side door.

Later that night, over dinner, Jimmy told Papa Joe the story.

His father shook his head. "Damn, Jimmy, your mom would have roasted you if she ever heard of you walking out on a girl. However, I would have done the same thing as you, given the circumstances."

Before going to bed, Jimmy took out his leather journal and wrote another letter to his mom.

Dear Mom,

I went on a first date with someone. Would you believe she brought a friend without telling me? Then, she expected me to be okay with paying for all three of us! She figured it would be okay, because she had gotten away with it in the past. I hope you won't be mad at me. I paid the bill and left after I pretended to go to the bathroom. I sure hope this was a one-off experience, and not the way dating is now. Even with the new technology, I think dating now is going to be harder than it was in your day.

Chapter 3: Spreading Their Wings

In the fall of 2007, Lauren was eager to spread her wings and fly. It didn't take her long to get fully immersed in college life, including getting involved with some of the university committees and clubs. Every week on Sunday, she would call her dad to catch him up.

"Hi, honey. How are you doing? What's the latest news?" Finn was so excited to talk to his little one that he was almost shouting.

"Hi, Dad. I'm all settled into my classes. So far, the professors seem to be pretty good. My roommate is okay. I think we will get along just fine. We don't have any classes together, though. She is a Forestry major."

"Wow, fantastic. Are you eating all right and not pizza every night?"

Dripping with sarcasm, she replied, "Yes, Dad."

They both laughed. Her father could picture her rolling her eyes at him.

"Oh, get this, Dad," Lauren continued. "I am going to be on the University Building Design Advisory Committee."

"Wow, sweetie. That happened fast! How did you swing that?"

"I know, right? One of my professors was talking about it in class this week. It sounded fun, so I threw my name in the hat and got chosen."

"I have a feeling that you are going to learn a lot from it, and it will look good on your resume, as well. As your father, I am always worried about you, but I am also excited that you seem to have found your stride."

"Hey, Dad, I gotta go. The study group for my textiles class is meeting for dinner. I love you and I miss you."

"I love you, too. Talk soon!"

* * * * *

A few weeks later, at one of their regular check-ins, Lauren blurted out, "Dad, do you remember when you told me there will always be that one goldbricker in a class?"

"Yeah, I do."

"Well, I met her, and she is in a few of my classes. Her name is Amber, and she is certainly here on the Daddy Scholarship Program." She could feel her dad's eyes roll right through the phone.

"Oh, geez. What did she do?"

"We have an Intro to Design class together. This week, our professor was showing us slides of interior design fails. They were all pretty funny.

"However, one showed a red carpet being in a bathroom. The whole class cringed out loud. This girl, Amber, spoke up and asked what was wrong with it. She said, 'It might feel nice on your cold toes.'"

Lauren had to hold the phone away from her ear for moment as her dad's laughter bellowed through the phone. "Lauren, sweetie, that was the funniest thing I've heard all day. I love you and miss you more."

Her dad sounded a little sad that he had to hang up the phone.

Lauren and Finn kept up their weekly check-ins all the way from the 2007-2008 college year until Lauren graduated in the spring of 2011.

* * * * *

When the end of summer of 2007 came, nearly every evening, Jimmy and Papa Joe could be found on the patio having their usual after-dinner drink and talking about their day.

"So, Jimmy, it sure looks like you were staying busy with the handyman stuff this summer. What do you think? Maybe you wanna give it a go?"

"I was thinking about that, too, this week. It was fun and I liked the idea of helping people do things that they couldn't—or shouldn't. The money wasn't bad either. The freedom of not having a regular nine-to-five job and not having to wear a suit is also appealing."

Jimmy rocked back in his chair as he took a long pull on his beer.

"I also figured out there were some things that I don't know, which I would need to learn about. I had to give up some jobs that seemed simple, but because I didn't have any plumbing or electrical experience for those, I turned 'em down. One of my clients, who is a Realtor, even suggested that I get licensed as a Home Inspector. He said the money is really good, it's fairly easy work, and the market here is starting to get really busy."

Papa Joe turned to look at his son. "I think that is a fantastic idea. Anytime you can add to your skill set, you become more valuable. I also want to tell you that I am mighty proud of you and the man you have become. If she were still here, I know your Mom would be bragging on you to all of her friends, for sure."

Papa Joe raised his bottle and Jimmy met it with his. The bottles clanked together.

"Thanks, Dad. I needed to hear that."

* * * * *

Jimmy connected with the local community college to start taking night classes in the trades he need more knowledge in.

During each semester of the 2007-2008 college year, he would have time for two classes. In his four classes, he would learn more about electrical, plumbing, carpentry, and construction basics.

Jimmy did well in all classes because he actually wanted to be there and learn.

* * * * *

Dear Mom,

It's fall now and the handyman thing seems to get busier every week. I have started to take some night classes in plumbing and electrical to start, and I'll take more later on. I still think about you a lot but I am not as sad anymore.

I heard a song on the radio that was one of your favorites: "Good Hearted Woman." I remember you teaching me how to dance in the kitchen. Then, every time we heard that song, we would go dance in the kitchen. I was sad that when I went to the kitchen this time, you weren't there.

I have slowed up on the girl goal for a little bit. If it's supposed to happen, then it will.

* * * * *

In the second semester of Lauren's 2007-2008 college year, Lauren experienced the Amber entitlement again.

It was during a lecture-only class on design history. The professor had a reputation for being tough and was a stickler for being on time to his class.

Amber, still thinking she could do no wrong, tested his patience one day. The squeaky side door gave her away as she tried to sneak in 30 minutes late.

Professor McNally stopped speaking and the class went silent for the longest minute.

"Ms. Amber, you are thirty minutes late to my class." He boomed. "You know the rules. I don't even know why you bothered to show up."

"Yes, but it wasn't my fault. There was this—"

The professor cut her off promptly. "I do not want to hear your lame excuse. If you can't be punctual to class, how to you expect to be punctual in the real world? You need to apologize to the class for cutting into their precious learning time with your drama."

In a barely genuine fashion, she whispered to the class, "I'm so sorry."

Professor McNally boomed again. "Now, leave. You'd better be more prepared on Wednesday."

* * * * *

From 2007 to 2011, Jimmy's friend, Calvin, also went to college, working through his teaching degree. He decided to minor in Industrial Arts. Calvin had always enjoyed building things and this gave him a chance to explore his more creative side.

The first time he struck an arc in his welding class, in 2008, he was hooked. As he started welding in his parents' garage, he happily discovered his artistic side. He loved to see what he could make out of scrap metal and things he collected from junkyards. Fortunately, his parents supported his new hobby and didn't mind letting Calvin fill the garage with his creations. They didn't use the garage much anyway.

Once a month, Calvin gathered up his projects and headed to the local farmer's market to see if they would sell. Sometimes they did. More times than not, people stopped by just to meet Gracie, his Golden Retriever.

Gracie was two years old when Calvin adopted her. She came from a home where the previous owner had passed away and the remaining family was not able to care for her. Calvin saw the "rescue" post in his Facebook news feed one day in 2008. He messaged the lady and set up a meet-and-greet. As soon as Calvin walked up the driveway, Gracie saw him and started wagging her tail wildly. They bonded immediately and Calvin took her with him nearly every place he went.

* * * * *

While his friend, Calvin, spent four years completing his teaching degree, Jimmy spent the same years taking classes—and acquiring various contracting licenses.

Jimmy even had a website created that advertised his business, Classic Handyman Service.

Jimmy and Calvin saw each other and spoke on occasion, but both young men focused on their careers.

After Calvin graduated in 2011, he got a job teaching Industrial Arts at one of the high schools. Jimmy continued to grow his popularity as a handyman.

* * * * *

Over the next few years, from 2011 to 2014, as Jimmy gained additional certifications and licenses, he was able to charge his clients more money. His investments into himself, his education, and his business were finally paying off. He and Papa Joe no longer had to struggle financially, and Jimmy even started saving.

Chapter 4: Squeaky Cabinets

In 2011, in her final semester of her four-year program, Lauren was the team leader in her class called Architectural Modeling. Lauren had minored in Structural Engineering, and learning about architecture was a component of that.

She had a good team but there is always that one person who tries to slide through with little work as possible. On her team, it was a girl named Amanda. Just as in the past, Amanda missed the weekly team meeting at the Campus Coffee Café—or "C Cubed," as they affectionately called it.

Lauren started the meeting without her.

"Hey, y'all, we need to talk about Amanda. Of course, she isn't here and our project due date is quickly approaching."

Paul said, "That ain't right. We all need this to graduate, and she has me worried about it. I can't afford another semester. I am strapped as it is."

Jorge put in his thoughts as well.

"I know this stuff goes on in the real world, but not on my watch. I work too hard to support a goldbricker. But what do we do? This is college."

Melissa had an idea.

"Hey, why don't we fire her?"

"Oooooh," Lauren rubbed her chin thoughtfully. "That's a helluva good idea. My dad taught me that in business, you gotta drop the dead weight. I'll have a chat with the professor after class today. Okay, that's settled. Let's get back to work."

The next day, they had an emergency meeting in the cafe.

Lauren got right to it.

"Okay, y'all. I will make this quick. I spoke with the professor and she agrees with us. It's going to be a tough lesson for Amanda. I get the idea that many people don't tell her 'No.' We can talk to her after class. Is there anything else we need to discuss?"

The rest of the group shook their heads.

"Okay. I gotta go. See ya in class tomorrow. This is going to be fun." She rubbed her hands together as she mocked an evil laugh.

The next day, Lauren leaned over and whispered to Amanda halfway through class.

"Hey, don't leave right away after class. We need to talk to you."

Amanda rolled her eyes at her. "Yeah, okay, whatever."

A small smile crept across Lauren's face as she turned back around. *This is going to be fun,* she thought to herself.

When the class was dismissed, the team met Amanda in the back of the classroom. The professor was still at her desk up front clearing up some paperwork and keeping an eye on the group.

With her hands on her hips and a smirk on her face, Amanda asked. "So, what's this all about? I have stuff to do, so you better make it fast."

Lauren smiled at her as the rest of the team stared directly at her.

"Oh, it will be. This is about you not pulling your weight and us having to cover for you, just to stay on schedule. The team voted and the professor has given us permission to fire you. You will have to talk to her about your options from here."

The smirk quickly disappeared from Amanda's face. "You can't do this. Do you know who my Daddy is?"

Lauren smiled at her again. "As a matter of fact, I do. He and I serve on the same university committee. If he asks me about it, I will be happy to tell him the truth. That had no sway in our decision."

Amanda fidgeted as she finally realized they were serious.

Melissa chimed in. "We are leaving on spring break now. We are all caught up, no thanks to you."

Jorge looked at Amanda with a grin. "Welcome to the real world, Amanda. This has been a fine example of 'Fuck around and find out.'"

In unison, the team turned on their heels and left the classroom. Once the door had shut behind them, they all looked at each other with big eyes.

Then, they burst out laughing.

Melissa was grinning. "Oh, my God, did you see her face?"

Paul added, "I know, right? Remind me not to get on Lauren's bad side. She doesn't mess around! Y'all have a great week. I am headed for Alaska for my spring break."

* * * * *

Two months later, Lauren and her team graduated with honors.

A month after that, she was hired by a boutique design firm in Seattle as their Interior Decorator. She worked with them for three years, from 2011 to 2014, on many beautiful historic buildings and mansions. Her crowning achievement was a huge, modern commercial building.

Lauren was named the top Interior Designer in the Seattle area. She liked Seattle and all of its hustle and bustle, but every day on her drive to work, she hoped she would see more of the sun. Lauren loved the work that she was doing but over the three years that she was in the northwest, the always-gloomy skies began to take a mental toll on her.

One Friday, she had a fantastic idea. "I miss seeing the sun and I am so tired of this gloomy sky all the time. I'm gonna go find some nicer weather," she declared to herself.

She packed a bag, told her boss that she had to leave for a couple of weeks, and went on a road trip. There was no real destination in mind. She simply figured her heart would tell her where to go.

She followed Highway 101 all the way down to California, stopping whenever the mood struck her.

She spent a day just driving through Redwoods National Park. She cruised through the famous Avenue of the Giants and even drove through the popular tunnel that was built through a tree trunk—California Tunnel Tree in Yosemite National Park.

A week later, the highway finally ended in Los Angeles. She stopped for the night and made the final six-hour push into her hometown in Phoenix the next day.

She was giddy with anticipation. She couldn't wait to surprise her dad.

When she was 10 minutes away, she stopped to text him, just to make sure he was home.

'Hey, Dad, how are ya? Just checking in. How are things? Whatcha doing?'

'Hey, honey, I'm just lounging around, watching golf. You good?'

A few minutes later, she was smiling as she quietly rolled into the driveway.

BONG! BONG!

The huge chimes could be heard all over the house.

"Leave it on the doorstep. I will get it later," her dad boomed from inside the house.

"Oh, but sir, you need sign for this." Lauren tried to disguise her voice as she yelled through the door.

The large oak door creaked as he opened it. He stood, frozen, with his mouth open as his brain tried processed what his eyes were seeing.

"Hi, Dad. I'm home." Lauren had the biggest smile on her face.

The big Irish man burst out crying as he pulled his only daughter into his arms.

"Oh, my God, you're here. What on earth? What are you doing here?" He struggled to get the words out of his mouth fast enough. He pushed her back to his arm's length.

"Let me get a good look at you. My little girl is all grown up now. You could not have made an old man happier. Come in! Come in!"

Lauren had tears running down her cheeks as she stepped over the threshold of her old home. It was nice to be home again.

* * * * *

Bing-bong!

Jimmy rang the doorbell of Dr. Alex's house.

Just as the doctor answered the door, Jimmy sneezed.

"Ah-choo!" Jimmy buried his nose in his sleeve. Again, "Ah-choo!" Jimmy looked up with watery eyes at the doctor.

"Bless you."

"Oh, my God, Doctor Alex, I am so sorry. I came by to take a look at your fence."

"Helluva greeting there, Jimmy," Doc said, chuckling. "Sounds like you still have that sniffle. The over-the-counter allergy meds aren't helping?"

"This week, it's been bad. I hate sneezing in a customer's house. It just seems rude to me. No, I've tried all the ones you recommended, but nothing lasts very long."

"Let's go check out that fence. Before you leave, I'll give you the name of a great allergy doctor. You will like her. Mention my name and her staff will get you right in."

"Fantastic. Thanks, Doc."

* * * * *

On the day of his appointment, Jimmy rolled up to the allergy doctor's office.

He got excited when he saw an old Craftsman-style home that had been converted into office space. He loved old homes and was happy that this one had not been torn down just to put something cookie-cutter in its place.

As Jimmy opened the front door, old-fashioned chimes alerted the staff to his arrival. He was soon signed in and waiting in the lobby, thumbing through an old magazine.

A few minutes later, a very good-looking woman wearing a business suit breezed through the front door. The staff seemed to know her fairly well and she headed through the waiting room door without even stopping. She was probably a pharmaceutical rep there on business.

How cool would it be if she ended up being my doctor?

As quickly as Jimmy had that thought, he had an answer. Under his breath, he said to himself, "Jimmy, you ain't that lucky."

Finally, the nurse called him back and led him to one of the examination rooms. It looked like every other doctor's exam room with the dull white paint, sailboat-on-a-lake artwork, linoleum floor, and the tiniest stainless-steel sink ever.

The nurse instructed him to take his shirt off while she took his vitals. After a few more standard questions, she said the doctor would be right in.

Many minutes and another old magazine later, there was a quiet knock on the door. Much to his surprise, the drug rep turned out to be Dr. Stephanie.

He stood up to shake her hand.

"You don't have to get up for me," she said with a smile. "It's nice to meet you."

Jimmy replied with a smile of his own. "Yes, I do. My mother would be very upset at my manners if I did not."

"Your mama raised you right. That's nice to see."

Dr. Stephanie took the round whirly stool and sat down. "So, what's got you coming to see me today?"

"This year has been a little tougher on allergies than I can recall. My doctor said I should come see you to get this figured out. I'm a handyman by trade, so I'm in a lot of homes and yards all week. Having the sniffles is really annoying, especially when it's in someone else's house. I can only imagine they are thinking that it's gross."

Dr. Stephanie assured him that he was in good hands as she explained the tests and procedures that she was about to put him through. After she was done with all of the poking and prodding, she had him sit up and she would return in 15 minutes to see the results on his back.

He was starting to feel a few parts tingle. The good-looking nurse checked in on him to see how he was doing and brought him a bottle of water. Ten minutes later, Dr. Stephanie came back in.

After examining his back and making some notes, she spoke up.

"Jimmy, it looks like you are allergic to almost every type of tree and grass outside. It's not a bad thing, and it's common. I have a few solutions for you. The first one is a series of shots. You would drop in once a day for about thirty days. We give you a shot and wait twenty minutes for any reaction. The shots help build your tolerance each day."

As much as he would have loved to come in every day just to see the beautiful doctor, that wasn't going to work with his busy schedule.

"The second option is a daily pill. It will take about a week to get up to full potency, and it will do the trick, for sure. No more sniffles."

A sly smile flashed across his face.

"Doc, I have a serious question for you." He paused for a few moments.

"Yes?" she answered, a serious look on her face.

"Are you putting me on the pill?" He held his straight face as long as he could. Ten long seconds of dead silence went by. Finally, he couldn't hold it anymore and a huge grin spread across his face. She realized that she had been had and burst out laughing.

She then scribbled out his prescription and handed it to him.

"Seriously, though, thanks for all your help. I'll get this going today. If you ever need a handyman here or at your house, let me know. I am one of the best in town." He handed her his card and went on his way.

Jimmy got home after visiting the drugstore. He told his dad about his adventure with the pretty doctor.

Papa Joe laughed, "Maybe I should get the sniffles, too. A good-looking woman could do me some good right now."

He closed his eyes, threw his head back, and sniffed the air a few times. Father and son looked at each other and cracked up laughing.

* * * * *

A few days later, Lauren was puttering around her dad's house in a restless sort of way.

Her dad boomed at her from his study. "Lauren, my dear, come on in here and have a seat."

Lauren entered and sat.

"It seems that something is bothering you." He stood up, turned on the espresso machine, and drew two espressos. He handed her one before sitting down in his recliner.

"Dad, I'm torn. I really like my job and the people that I work with but the Seattle environment is always so drab and gloomy. I can't remember the last time I saw a sunny sky there."

Her dad took a sip and raised an eyebrow. "And...?"

"Like I said, I like it there but the lack of sun is killing my soul."

He nodded in agreement. "I hear you. Let me ask you this…"

"Yeah?"

"When you got your degree, you told me you could work anywhere you wanted, right?"

"Yeah."

"And now you have the degree and some pretty impressive projects under your belt, right?"

"Yes."

"Don't you think you could easily work wherever you wanted to, even back here at home? Maybe even open your own design studio? I'm sure there is plenty of work to be had here in the Valley."

Lauren rocked back in her chair and twisted her hair around her finger, just like she did every time she was deep in thought. She already knew the answer deep inside her, but up until now, she was afraid to say it out loud. It had been on her mind for quite some time.

"Eureka!"

She sat up so quickly in her chair that her espresso cup almost tipped over.

"Eureka? Who says that?" asked her dad with a puzzled look on his face.

Lauren laughed.

"Yeah, I have always wanted to say that and this seemed like the perfect time to use it. I know what I am going to do!"

Her dad rolled his eyes and then a big smile appeared on his face like he knew what she was going to say before she said it.

"Oh, yeah, what's that?"

"I'd like to come back to Phoenix and open my own studio."

"My darling daughter, I cannot think of anything that would make me happier, and you, too. What can I do to help out?"

Lauren grinned as they began talking about it.

The next few days were a whirlwind of brainstorming and planning the next phase of her design career. She wanted to get as much done before her return trip to Seattle.

On her last day there, her dad called her into his study again.

"I have a surprise for you, before you go." He tossed over a set of keys and an envelope.

"You are going to need a place to live. This was your mother's house before we got married. We just never had the heart to sell it. Secretly, I hoped that we would one day be able to give it to you. You should drive by it on your way out of town. It's in the Moon Valley area, in an old, well-established neighborhood. See if you like it or not."

Lauren was speechless. Tears started running down her cheeks as she ran over to hug her father.

"I love you so much. I could not have asked for a better dad."

* * * * *

It didn't take Lauren long to round up her business in Seattle and make the move back to Phoenix. She had only been in her "new" house a few weeks and was already highly annoyed by her squeaky kitchen cabinets. She tried every trick she could think of, including using lubricant spray and rubber bands. The cabinet doors still didn't close quite right and sounded like a horror movie when they opened. It wasn't like she was going to disturb anyone else in the house, given that she lived alone, but it grated on her engineering sense as subpar. Her solution: she needed a handyman, and she needed one right now.

She found Jimmy's website online, along with a few other sites. The others seemed a little too flashy for a handyman, while Jimmy's was simple and straightforward. Jimmy's just seemed to speak to her. Of course, she did her due diligence and checked him out with the licensed contractor site and a general web search about him. He had good reviews. She also noticed that he was very handsome... and blond. She had a thing for blonds. Just to be thorough, she looked up his social media details. She had a feeling he wasn't much of the social media type, so it didn't surprise her that she didn't find much.

Jimmy's phone rang.

"Classic Handyman Service, this is Jimmy."

"Hi, Jimmy, this is Lauren Perry, and I got your number from your website. I need your help.

"Sure, tell me what's going on."

"I have a few kitchen cabinets that are squeaking and won't close properly. I have tried every trick I know. When can I get on your schedule to come check it out?"

Jimmy paused for a moment while he checked his calendar. "I can come by tomorrow at three. What's your address?"

They exchanged the address details and hung up.

* * * * *

Jimmy arrived at Lauren's house right on time, as always. He had sometimes gotten business because the previous handyman arrived too late or not at all. For him, being late and making someone wait is one of the rudest things someone can do.

He rang the doorbell.

Within a moment, a woman opened the door. The first things he noticed were her beautiful red hair and freckles. They locked eyes for just a moment, and Jimmy's memory flashed back to the day he saw the redheaded girl in the coffee shop after graduation. *Nah, it couldn't' be,* he told himself.

Upon opening the door, Lauren also stopped. He was really tall and had wavy blond hair. She couldn't pull herself away from his blue eyes fast enough to not get caught staring. Her heart skipped a beat. He was even cuter in person. She also thought that she had seen him somewhere before but could not place him.

He shyly blinked himself back to reality and introduced himself.

"I'm Jimmy, the handyman. You must be Lauren?" He held his hand out.

She extended her hand to shake his. "Yes, I am. Thanks so much for coming."

Jimmy warmly shook it, and thought he felt some sparks fly. Lauren then invited him in and showed him to the kitchen and the problem doors. Jimmy's head was on a swivel as he looked around the house. "Wow, you have a really great house."

"Thanks, it was my mom's house before she married my dad. Sometimes, I think about selling it. But I'm sentimental. I get that from my dad. Besides, it's too much fun changing around the rooms whenever I want to. That's what I do, I am an Interior Designer. I minored in Structural Engineering, too."

Jimmy was liking her more and more. He felt that they spoke the same language. "That's really great. I have been in a few homes that could have used your touch, for sure." He laughed. "There was this house last year with pink wallpaper and red carpet in the bathroom." Lauren covered her mouth in mock horror, then started laughing.

"Oh, I could tell you stories, too! Maybe I should write a book."

"Oh, I don't doubt it," Jimmy replied with a knowing laugh.

"Here's the worst door. I've tried all the hacks I can think of, and the doors just kept laughing at me. I'll let you do your thing. If you need me, I will be in my office down the hallway. There is cold water and soda in the blue fridge. Help yourself!"

"Thank you. I will."

In her kitchen, she had a regular fridge for the household and a separate bright blue retro fridge for sodas, beer, etc. It was just like her—fun, and just a wee bit off the normal path. She headed toward her office.

Jimmy jiggled the doorknob and checked the hinges. He got some tools from his truck, and had it working smoothly within ten minutes.

He then fixed the other cabinet doors that needed a little bit of attention.

When he was finished, he wandered down the oak-planked hallway. He came upon an open door, spotted Lauren sitting at a desk, and knocked.

"Hi, your kitchen cabinets are done. Just like new."

Her face lit up. She turned in her chair and saw he had a smudge of dirt on his cheek. She smiled and followed him into the kitchen. She tried the cabinet doors out and became excited.

"Thank you so much!" Lauren gushed as she wrote him a check for his services.

"You're very welcome! By the way, for some reason, you look familiar to me. Have we met somewhere before?"

"No, I don't think so. I would have remembered. I get told that a lot, I must have one of those faces." She smiled back at Jimmy.

"Okay, I just had to ask."

Jimmy smiled as he left a few cards on the kitchen counter and picked up his check. "Thanks for the business. I really do appreciate it. If you need anything else, please don't hesitate to call me. You have the coolest house on the block."

Jimmy headed home. Lauren was his last appointment for the day, and he could not get her out of his mind. He met his dad on the porch, as usual, with a beer, to catch up and talk about their day.

Jimmy told his dad about his last job. Papa Joe saw the excitement in his son's eyes as he talked about Lauren.

After dinner and cleaning up the kitchen, Jimmy had some quiet time to himself.

From the desk drawer in his room, he pulled out his leather journal.

> *Dear Mom,*
>
> *I met a woman today. She was a new client. I think she might be the same girl I saw in the coffee shop a long time ago. I didn't talk to her then. Anyway, I got this funny feeling in my gut that I don't know what to do with. I can't stop thinking of her. She's an interior designer and knows about structural engineering. We can talk the same talk.*

Anyway, Mom, I'm rambling but I thought you should know. I miss you.

Chapter 5: The Collaboration Begins

Several weeks went by, and as busy as Jimmy was, he could not seem to get thoughts of Lauren out of his head. That wasn't normal for him. He had forgotten about what those feelings felt like and it was a little scary. He was hoping that she would call again with something else to fix in her house.

On the other side of town, Lauren couldn't stop thinking about the tall, cute handyman that fixed her cabinet doors. Somehow, she knew that if she was going to see him again, she would have to call him.

Maybe something would "accidentally, on purpose" break. She didn't have to wait long.

The next morning, she walked into the bathroom and stepped in about an inch of chilly water.

"Ah shit!" Lauren jumped as the icy water hit her bare feet.

It appeared that the supply hose to the toilet had split overnight. Water was everywhere. She was glad it was just the hose. She reached for the valve to turn it off, then grabbed a towel to dry her feet. She headed to her office to call Jimmy. She quietly smiled to herself that she had a good reason to call him back.

"Hi, Jimmy? This is Lauren Perry. You fixed my kitchen cabinets a few weeks ago."

"Ah, yes, Lauren, how are you doing? Is everything okay?"

"Not really. I have a bigger problem now."

"Oh? What's going on?" He grabbed a pad to start taking notes.

"Overnight, the toilet supply hose broke and there is water all over the bathroom floor. It's even seeping into the hallway carpet."

"Damn. I can be there first thing this morning. I know this is silly, but I have to ask, did you turn off the valve?"

In a somewhat exasperated voice, because she is an engineer who knows about this stuff, replied, "Yes, of course." She then realized it's a valid question and didn't spend another second on it.

"Okay, good. Let me gather a few things. I'll be right over. Do you have an idea of how long that broken hose is? I wanna make sure I bring the right size with me."

"I believe it is twelve inches."

About an hour later, Jimmy knocked on the door.

Lauren opened the door wearing jeans and a white tank top. Her hair was in a ponytail and her feet were bare. He did a double-take and tried to hide it.

She noticed it and gave him a small, playful smile.

"Good morning. Thank you for showing up so quickly!"

"No problem. I have learned over the last few years to make some wiggle room in my daily schedule for these kinda things… because shit happens."

Jimmy smiled and followed her down the hall to the calamity of the day.

Jimmy grimaced as he inspected the broken hose. He was not used to seeing a woman's bathroom. He scanned the counter. It was full of bottles, jars, and brushes. He wrinkled up his face like he had just bitten a lemon but he did not conceal his expression in time. Lauren noticed.

"What? Haven't you seen a woman's bathroom before?" She started laughing.

"What are all those—"

"Jimmy, don't you dare finish that question," she said, laughing and wagging a finger at him.

He set down his toolbox, a fan, and the new steel braided hose he brought with him. As he got to work, Lauren watched from the doorway, trying not to stare at the cute guy in jeans on his knees in her bathroom—and to not look obvious about it.

Without looking up, Jimmy asked, "Hey, could you hand me that crescent wrench?"

"Of course, do you want the six-inch or eight-inch one?" He could hear the smile in her voice and turned his head just in time to see her blush. She was trying to stifle a giggle. He rolled his eyes at her and chuckled. "Oh, someone's got jokes."

Lauren laughed and headed downstairs, saying she was going to make breakfast.

After about 30 minutes, he was done cleaning up and drying out what he could.

He went to the kitchen to let her know he was finished.

"I'm going to leave you one of my floor fans. It will help dry out the carpet. If you let the water sit, you'll get mold pretty quickly."

"Fantastic. Thank you so much. I just made a fresh pot of coffee. Would you like a cup?"

Lauren had a feeling in her gut about him and didn't want him to leave yet. After thinking about it for a while, she realized that he also looked familiar, but couldn't place him.

"Oh, that's the magic word, right?" Jimmy grinned. "I would love a cup. Cream and sugar, please."

Jimmy sat down at the kitchen table while Lauren prepared two cups of coffee. She also put a plate of cookies and muffins out. After she sat down, it was awkwardly quiet for a few moments while they enjoyed those first sips of coffee.

Lauren was the first to break the silence. "So, I don't see a wedding ring on your finger. Are you married? Do you have any kids? What's the scoop on you?"

Jimmy's coffee nearly went down the wrong way. He tried not to spit out his coffee on her as he stopped himself from choking. She had caught him off-guard.

Lauren turned red as she realized the words were out of her mouth before she could stop them. "Oh, my God, I am so sorry for being blunt and nosy like that."

Jimmy finally caught his breath and laughed.

"It's okay. It's a valid question. I just wasn't expecting it to come so soon from you. To be fair, I am curious about you, too. Since you opened the door, we may as well go through it. I'll go first." Jimmy was never one to back up from a challenge or a fair question.

Jimmy continued, "I am not married, nor do I have any kids. I've been single now about five years. One ex tried to trick me into having kids and I just didn't want them. Had she been more upfront at the beginning about that, I wouldn't have asked her out on a date." Jimmy took a bite of a cookie. "Your turn now."

"I've been single for about two years. We weren't married, just dating. This was back when I lived in Seattle. It wasn't a horrible breakup. We just realized that we had drifted apart and wanted different things out of our lives.

"I also knew a long time ago that I didn't want kids and wasn't the mom type. Kids are okay, but I just don't want my own. A lot of people, including my dad gave me a lot of crap about that. It's none of their damn business.

My dad, being the good Irish Catholic he is, wanted to know when we were going to get married and when he could expect grandkids. My dad has always been very churchy. I wasn't, and still am not."

Jimmy nodded his head and knew where she was coming from. "So, what did you tell him?"

Lauren laughed at the thought of what was coming next.

"Well, two strong Irish people can play that game. I loved giving my dad smart-ass responses, when it came to religion. He was way too much into the Kool-Aid as far as I was concerned. I told him it was so we could have sex and take advantage of the tax deduction."

Jimmy laughed so hard at that he banged the table and coffee flew out of his cup. He thought to himself, *Yes, she is a feisty one. I kinda like that.* That little warm feeling from a few weeks ago was starting to grow again.

Jimmy spoke up. "So, you moved right into this house after moving back here?"

"Yes. It was my mother's before she was married. She died when I was ten. My dad just never had the heart to let it go. It's paid off, so I only have taxes and insurance to pay on it. For just me, it seems a little big sometimes. In the summer, I shut down about half the rooms so I don't have to air-condition them. I could probably make a tidy sum if I were to sell it, but it somehow keeps me connected with my mom."

Jimmy refilled his coffee from the carafe on the table. "I lost my mom, too, when I was seventeen. I still live with my dad. After my mom died, he needed some looking after because he is in a wheelchair most of the time. Now that I'm an adult, we consider ourselves 'roommates.' He's pretty cool to have as a roommate. We have gotten a lot closer than how we were when I was younger. I was looking at the pictures on the wall in your office. Are those from previous projects?"

Lauren nibbled at a muffin before she answered. "Those were projects that were special to me because I got to help with the building design. As I mentioned when we first met, in addition to being an interior designer, I also minored in structural engineering."

Jimmy let out a low whistle.

"I remember you telling me that. That was some good work you did there. Speaking of houses, I had probably better get rolling toward the next job on today's agenda. Thanks for the work. The coffee was really great. I really do appreciate it."

Jimmy headed for the kitchen door where his truck was parked just outside on the driveway.

"You are welcome. I really appreciate you coming so quickly." Lauren got up and saw him out.

As he drove away, he could still see her waving from the kitchen door.

While having dinner later that day, He told Papa Joe about Lauren and the leak in her bathroom.

Joe looked at him with a silly grin on his face. "It seems you were there a while. That must have been some big leak."

Jimmy got a little red, knowing his dad was teasing him.

"Well, she made coffee—and good coffee at that. I couldn't say no."

Joe pressed on, "What did you find out? Is she married, divorced, kids? She made you coffee, really? She must really like you."

Jimmy scoffed.

"What do you mean, *like* me? She was just being nice."

Joe rolled his wheelchair over to where Jimmy was standing.

"No, son, being nice is paying you on time, and maybe giving you a tip. She likes you and wants to get to know more about you."

"Are you sure?"

"Look, this old man has been around the block a few times, and trust me, I think she really likes you. And she should. You're a damn fine catch. You just watch."

"But she is a client. Isn't it bad to date a client or customer? What if it goes sideways? If that happens, then you've lost a client, and that's not good, especially one with such a cool house—and lots of return work, I am sure."

"Oh, yeah, certainly in Corporate America it's a bad thing, but it still goes on. But you are both business owners and maybe there is a chance for something greater here. My advice is that it's worth exploring and to not rush into it. I haven't met her yet, but if she is anything like what I think she is like, you'd better not let go of this one."

"Okay, Dad, I will keep my eyes open. I think I like her too and don't wanna do something stupid by moving too fast."

* * * * *

Dear Mom,
I can't believe she called back. At least I know I didn't creep her out. She actually made coffee and we chatted. Not like first date

stuff, which I don't even want to think about yet, but a real conversation. She is pretty damn smart. Maybe there is something to this?

* * * * *

A few weeks later, Jimmy took a call from one of his more eccentric customers, Mrs. Marsh, a trust fund baby who was heavily involved with volunteering at the local animal shelter and provided funds for animal welfare around town.

In her large, ranch-style home, was a zoo of various animals she rescued, including four cats that had come into the animal shelter, whom she just couldn't say no to.

"Jimmy? This is Mrs. Marsh over on Why Worry Lane. How are you and your dad doing?"

"Hi, Mrs. Marsh. Dad and I are doing just fine. What do you have going on? Is there anything wrong with the house?"

"Oh, that's good to hear. Oh, no, nothing is wrong with the house, but I do have a project that I want to discuss with you. When can you come by? It's pretty involved."

"Really? I can make it out there later this afternoon, after my last job. Would that work for you? What kind of project did you have in mind?"

Mrs. Marsh let out a hearty laugh, "Oh, Jimmy, that is going to be part of the surprise! I just can't wait to see what you think about this one."

Jimmy hung up the phone. He had helped her out in the past with a few of her wild ideas for improvements around the house.

For example, there was a laundry chute from her upstairs bedroom all the way into the downstairs laundry room. There was an indoor dog park that included a water fountain as part of the dog's water bowl. In the kitchen, she had a water cooler that pulled out from its own cabinet near the fridge.

He really liked working on those projects. They were fun, and a challenge different from the same old stuff he had been fixing for people all over town.

Trumpets greeted him as he rang the doorbell button. Jimmy pushed on the big door into her house. She greeted him with a smile and a hug, as always.

"Jimmy, it is so good to see you. It's been a few moons since you were here last. How is your dad doing?" Mrs. Marsh repeated her earlier question. She was always concerned about Jimmy's dad because he was in a wheelchair.

"Hi, Mrs. Marsh. It *has* been a while. You look great and the house is looking good, too. Dad and I are doing just fine and have figured out this bachelor thing. I think Dad misses having a woman around the house, but he won't say it. What kind of crazy idea do you have this time?"

"I saw this video online the other day, showing a house that had cat tunnels and such all the way through the house, which even went from the first floor to the second floor. I was thinking I should do something like that!"

"No way, how cool!" Jimmy listened to her ideas and took some notes as they wandered through the expansive house.

He sat down at the kitchen table with his notepad to start sketching out some ideas. Mrs. Marsh put a cold beer in front of him. She knew he was done working for the day. He didn't say no and thanked her for it. He finished some rough sketches and took a few measurements before he headed for home.

A lightbulb went off in his head. This was the perfect opportunity to ask Lauren out for coffee. He could pick her brain for additional ideas. While he liked her, he still needed to be cautious with his heart. The last couple of girls he tried to date had not gone well.

* * * * *

Mid-morning the next day, Jimmy had just finished one job. His next one wasn't until later that afternoon.

It was a perfect time to see if Lauren had time for some coffee.

She picked up the phone on the second ring. "Hello. This is Lauren."

"Hey, Lauren, this is Jimmy. I hope I didn't catch you in the middle of something?"

"Nothing big, I was just catching up on paperwork. Nothing too exciting. Are you doing okay? What's up?"

"One of my more eccentric clients has some crazy ideas and I think I need your input as to how best to execute her plan. Do you have time for a coffee?"

"Oh, that sounds like it could be fun. What time do you wanna meet?"

"How about in a half an hour at The Coffee Stand?"

"I will see you there."

Once they had their coffee, Jimmy outlined the idea that Mrs. Marsh had for the cat tunnels and why he wanted her advice on the best place to put holes and tunnels in the walls. She was intrigued.

"The lady with the zoo in her house?"

"Yep, that's the one. Anyway, she wants to put cat runs all over her house, including tunnels to all the rooms between the floors and the basement. She even wants to see if I can integrate it with the dog park."

Lauren took a sip of her coffee as she gazed off into space for a few moments while she was processed the idea that Jimmy ran past her.

"Ya know, Jimmy," she finally said with a smile on her face, "that is not a half-bad idea. I wish I had thought of it sooner. From a customer's perspective, I can see it, and having known a few cats in my life, they would totally go for it. With the interior design element, I can help with that part for sure. On the business side for you, it makes even more sense. You can do more creative work for more money and less stress. You may fix a leaky faucet once in a while, but you could hire an assistant who wants to learn the biz and have him or her do those jobs.

"I even had another thought. If this takes off, we—I mean you—could be like that treehouse guy and go all over the country building these custom runs for people."

The excitement was brimming all over her face. Jimmy's ears perked up when he heard the "we" and shook his head.

"Yeah, right. Like that is going to happen. Let's not get ahead of ourselves just yet. One dream at a time! That last one is pretty damn big, by the way. Not sure I am ready for that yet. By the way, do you happen to like camping?"

"Yeah, I do. Why do you ask?"

"Oh, I was just wondering to see if you haven't been too citified that you can't get out in the woods once in a while." A big smile crossed his face.

"Oh, Mr. Jimmy, I will have you know that in my backyard is a travel trailer outfitted with all the goodies to stay off grid for at least a week." It was Jimmy's turn to be impressed. He didn't know what to say.

* * * * *

The following day, Jimmy and Lauren arrived at Mrs. Marsh's house.

Mrs. Marsh eyeballed Lauren with a big smile.

"Lauren, it is very nice to meet you. Your hair is beautiful. Jimmy didn't tell me he had a girlfriend and I've known him for a while." She slyly winked at Lauren who raised her eyebrows while giving her a wry smile.

"Now, Mrs. Marsh, she is not my girlfriend. She happens to be a fantastic interior designer that I met while doing some work on her own house. She knows about structural engineering, too. I brought her along to get her expert opinion on this," Jimmy interjected quickly.

"Oh, my goodness, Jimmy, I am so sorry for assuming. You know what they say about that…"

Mrs. Marsh paused, then continued.

"Anyway, Lauren, it's very nice to meet you. Jimmy is the best handyman in town. He's been helping me out for a while now." She tried her best to take her foot out of her mouth. "I better return to the kitchen to finish baking cookies for the orphanage. I take the kids cookies and milk every Friday afternoon. Y'all feel free to wander about as you see fit."

Lauren gave Mrs. Marsh a big hug. "Mrs. Marsh, it was lovely to meet you. You are certainly as nice as Jimmy said you are. I can see why you are one of his favorites. We will come find you when we are done."

Jimmy was already on his way to the living room when Mrs. Marsh leaned over to Lauren and whispered in her ear, "He's a good one, dear. Don't you dare let him get away."

She winked at Lauren. Lauren could feel her face get flushed.

As she caught up with Jimmy, he gave her a sideways glance and looked at her quizzically.

"What's wrong with your face? It looks red."

"Oh, nothing, just girl talk."

Jimmy just rolled his eyes and smiled at her. "Yeah, right."

As they walked through the house, it was Jimmy's turn for his face to turn red, as he started sneezing. He grabbed a few tissues from the bathroom and stuffed them in his pocket. He was taking his allergy meds regularly, but Mrs. Marsh did have a bunch of cats.

* * * * *

Later that night at dinner, Jimmy and Papa Joe were sitting around the table and catching up on the day's events. Joe finished his meal with a final swipe around the plate with some bread.

"Jimmy, that gravy was tasty. I think you must have gotten your cooking chops from your mom."

"Thanks, Dad. It's actually becoming fun to do, when earlier, I thought it was just going to be a pain in the butt." That reminded him of a memory of his mom when he was just seven years old.

It was Sunday morning at the crack of dawn. Little Jimmy woke up. It was his mom's birthday and he was feeling sad as he hadn't gotten her anything for a gift. He tried to make French toast for his mom for her birthday. It looked easy when she did it.

He made a huge mess cracking the first egg.

Prior to trying to crack some more, he plopped some butter in the frying pan and turned on the heat. He got busy soaking the bread and forgot about the pan heating up.

He set off the fire alarm with the now smoking-hot pan. He jumped and the soggy bread and bowl went everywhere except for in the pan.

Still in panic mode, he threw the smoking pan into the sink and sat down in the goo on the floor and started crying.

He was scared that his mom would be furious.

She came, running into the kitchen.

In the quietest voice, his mom asked, "Jimmy, what happened?"

In between sobs and sniffles, he explained he just wanted to make breakfast for her birthday. His poor little shoulders were still shaking as Emma pulled him into her lap and hugged him tight.

"Oh, Jimmy, it's okay, and I love that you tried. That's the present that I will always remember.

* * * * *

Papa Joe rolled onto the porch followed by Jimmy, who was carrying two glasses of bourbon. He locked his wheels as Jimmy placed their drinks on a table, then sat in his rocking chair.

"So, it looks like you and Lauren are becoming fast friends. How's that going? Do you think you fancy her yet?" Papa Joe reached for his glass.

"Well, shit, Dad. Mrs. Marsh mentioned something along those lines, too. What is up with you guys? Are you in cahoots to try and get me married off soon? I like Lauren, and she is nice and all that, but we are just working together on a few projects that are coming up. She knows stuff that I don't. Speaking of business, I was thinking about things on the way home today. What do you think about me hiring a helper? I have a funny feeling that if these special jobs start taking off, I won't have enough time to take care of my regular customers."

"Jimmy, that thought has also crossed my mind. I feel bad sometimes that when I call you, I am taking you off a job that is paying. The customers probably don't like it much either. Plus, it seems that you are busy enough that you could at least justify a part-time helper."

"I'll reach out to my buddy, Calvin. He teaches Industrial Arts at the high school down the street. Maybe there is a kid there who might want some real-life experience and put those skills to work. I'll give him a call this week and see what shakes out."

* * * * *

That Friday, he met his friend, Calvin, at the local pub for a beer. He told him about the project he was working on for Mrs. Marsh. Calvin got excited and thought he had the perfect student in mind for the job.

"By the way, how's the dating scene treating you lately?"

Calvin grimaced and took a long swig of his beer.

"Wow, that bad?" Jimmy said with a sad face.

"Man, it's not good. There are so many fakes out there, it's hard to tell who's real and who's not. There is one gal I like right now. Her name is Jennifer. We haven't met yet but we have had some good discussions online. I think I may see if she wants to meet me in real life. She lives in Colorado, though."

Jimmy smiled.

"Wow. That would be amazing. I hope she wants to come. As for me, I am not in a hurry. I've got Papa Joe to look after, and I seem to be getting busier now. If someone comes along, I'm certainly open to the idea of it."

"Hey! Don't I know you guys?"

A voice came from behind them, sounding oddly familiar. Jimmy and Calvin whipped their heads around to find their old high school friend, Alex, standing there.

"Holy crap! Alex, what's going on man?" Jimmy jumped up to give him a hug. Calvin was right behind him with his own hug. "Wow, how long has it been?"

"Oh, man, it's really good to see y'all too. Yeah, it's been a spell. Since graduation, I think. That was in 2007. It's 2014 now, so I guess it's been nearly seven years. Wow, time sure flies!"

Calvin said, "Hey, pull up a chair and tell us what you are up to these days."

Alex took a long pull on his beer. "Y'all remember when I used to steal cars?"

Jimmy and Calvin nodded their heads.

"Well, I got caught after a while and spent a few years in jail. I'm out now and being a good boy. However, you would not guess what I do for a living now."

Jimmy scrunched up his face like he was thinking. "Hmmm, no idea."

"You are going to love this. I am a repo man," Alex said with a laugh.

Jimmy and Calvin looked at each other and burst out laughing. "You're serious?"

"Yeah. Now, I get paid to steal them. If I had only known then." Alex chuckled and then proceeded to tell them how his parole officer put him in touch with a local auto recovery company that was looking to hire ex-cons. He got the job a few years ago and had been doing it ever since. He explained that he even started his own YouTube channel and gained 500 thousand followers because of weekly posts about the craziest repo of the week. Alex also explained that he decided to simply focus on rebuilding himself and his life, and that's why he hadn't gotten back in touch with anyone from high school.

Jimmy clapped Alex on the back and congratulated him.

Calvin did, too, then said, "I think it's time for a round of beers!"

The trio spent the next little while catching each other up on their lives and enjoying their reunion.

Chapter 6: Tears and Beers

After months of texting and numerous emails back and forth, Calvin and Jennifer finally decided to meet. Given that summer just started, it was the perfect time. Calvin was finished with the 2013-2014 school year and had two months of vacation time to fill.

It was just as scary a prospect for Calvin as it was for Jennifer. They had each been down this road before and the magic, sadly, didn't always transfer across from the inter-webs into the real world.

There was a lot riding on this weekend; so many layers of the onion to peel back and discover. The attraction was there, certainly, as was the desire... and what possibly might feel like love.

But Calvin couldn't stop himself from wondering.

What if she hogs the bathroom for an hour and I have to pee? Do we close the door or keep it open?

Calvin had always been a "close the door" kinda guy. Everyone knows what goes on in there—you just don't need to see it.

What if her hair clogs up the shower every week? What if we can't stand each other's voices?

Up to that point, they had not actually talked on the phone. She could end up sounding like that TV show nanny from back in the day. So, that could be a big surprise.

Jennifer thought about having each other make a video for the other. That way, they could hear their voices and make sure that one of them was not a "bot." But they never did.

Saturday finally arrived. He changed his clothes three times because he wasn't sure that she would like what he chose. He decided on a dress shirt with dressy-casual pants. He reached into the closet and selected a striped tie. Finally satisfied, he slipped into his penny loafers that still squeaked as he was walking out the door.

He drove around the airport parking lot until he found the perfect spot. Jennifer's flight was on time, and everything was going according to the meet-up plan. The gate finally opened, and the passengers started filing out. There were a few soldiers on board and their families ran up to greet them with tears and hugs.

Calvin stood, holding a dozen roses and a sign that he had made: "Jennifer, it's me, Calvin!" The stream of people continued to walk past him as he started getting that funny feeling that something was wrong. When the flight attendants walked past and shortly thereafter, the pilots came off, Calvin got worried. No Jennifer. His heart stopped beating as his sign and flowers dropped from his hands onto the carpet. She wasn't on the plane and there was no text or voicemail from her. Still somewhat hopeful, he waited in the chairs for another 30 minutes, continually checking his phone—to no avail. He loosened his tie as tears ran down his face. How could he have been fooled again?

He didn't care if anyone saw him cry. It wasn't about them at all. Why did he always trust people will do what they say they will do? He finally accepted that this was not going to happen. Calvin left the flowers and the sign on the waiting-area chairs and slowly walked away. This time, he did not look back.

As he trudged through the airport, he noticed a woman standing all by herself in an empty gate. She was tall, had beautiful blonde hair, and wore a skirt and blouse that could have come straight from a Paris runway.

A helium balloon was on the ceiling and the "Welcome" sign barely hung from her fingers. The tears on her face told the same story of what he just went through.

Calvin slowly walked toward her as she looked up. Somehow, she could feel that he had just had the same thing happen to him.

"I know that you don't know me, but it looks like we just experienced the same thing. Stood up, right?

She nodded.

"Can I give you a hug because I need one, too? My name is Calvin, by the way."

She held up her arms as tears started down Calvin's face again. They hugged for what seemed like forever. Finally, someone else understood the pain that he was feeling.

"My name is Melissa. I'm sorry we had to meet like this."

"Do you want to sit down?"

Melissa sat down and pulled a bottle of water out of her bag. After a long drink, she looked up at Calvin.

"The same thing just happened to you too?"

"Yeah. I'm sorry it happened to you. I thought this sort of thing only happens to nerds and geeks like me." He chuckled at his own joke and hoped that it would at least bring a half-smile for Melissa.

She looked him up and down. Eventually, a small smile appeared and she said, "Well, you are kinda nerdy, but that doesn't make it right."

Calvin's eyes opened wide. He did not expect her to make a joke at this time.

It got quiet as they looked at each other, then they burst out laughing. They were laughing so hard that people walking past them couldn't help but smile, too. Melissa stood up and held out her hand.

"Would you like to join me for a drink before we head out of this place and resume our lives?"

"I would be happy to." He took her hand and stood up.

They headed for the bar.

While they had lunch and swapped online dating stories, they decided to let themselves off the hook and be kind to themselves.

The bartender laid the tab on the table for them. Calvin picked it up immediately. Melissa protested. She wanted to pay for her share, because he was still just a stranger.

"Absolutely not, and I'll not hear another word of it. I am glad that I met you. You made a tragic day so much better than you know, and I can't thank you enough."

"Oh, no, it was *you* that rescued *me*. Now, I know that this seems cliché and all, but I want to give you my card just in case you feel like talking."

"Oh, wow, that's very nice of you. I hope that you are sure of this, because I might just take you up on it." Calvin grinned.

"I'm sure. Now get home safely. I hope your week gets better."

He didn't even remember the drive home.

Despite his lovely encounter, he was still numb from the disappointment and heartbreak.

He crashed on his bed without even bothering to change his clothes. His faithful Golden Retriever, Gracie, snuggled up next to him.

It was dusk when he woke up to someone knocking on his door.

Still sleepy-eyed, he padded to the front door. He opened it and a courier handed him an express delivery envelope before departing.

It was from Jennifer.

Calvin just stared at it. He didn't open it right away, fairly certain it was some bullshit excuse to not meet him, how it was all about her and not him.

A little while later, he fired up the coffee maker and added one more scoop than usual. After the first sip of strong brew passed his lips, he ripped open the envelope.

"I can't do this, and I hope you will be okay. Someday, maybe I will be able to explain it."

Aloud, Calvin exclaimed, "Well, shit, fire, and save the matches! I was hoping for a better explanation than that!"

He crumpled up and threw the letter across the room. He deserved a lot more of an explanation than that.

This was a little better than ghosting someone, but barely. But she tried, right? He had to give her that.

He sat down on the couch. Gracie jumped up right beside him. She laid her head in his lap as if she was trying to say that this will pass, and it will be okay.

"Well, now what, Gracie? Do I get back on that app or chill on this for a while?"

He didn't get an answer from Gracie, just a tail wag.

While he was in the shower, he came up with a fix for his predicament.

A three-day ride on his old Harley usually put everything right with the world. He was normally such a planner, but this time, he decided he would just let the wind blow him wherever it likes.

He packed a light bag and some provisions for Gracie. He noticed a calm had come over him and he felt at peace again. He knew that everything would be all right, eventually. It just sucked right now.

Jimmy called Calvin to see how meeting his mystery date went. Calvin told him what happened.

"Dude, I'm so sorry that happened. That sucks."

"Yeah, I know. Listen, I am going to get out of town for a few days and get some knees in the breeze. Can you keep an eye on my place? I'm taking Gracie with me."

"Of course. Have a great time. Let me know when you get back."

"I will. Thanks. I'll be by tomorrow morning to drop off the house key."

Chapter 7: A Man and His Dog

On Saturday morning, Calvin got Gracie into her harness and racing goggles. He lifted her into the motorcycle sidecar that he built specially for Gracie so she could go for rides with him. She loved the wind in her face and tongue hanging out the side of her mouth.

At least she wouldn't slobber on the bike, just maybe someone's windshield.

Her sidecar had a soft, non-slip grip bed inside and a windscreen for when the wind got too much for her. There was even a spill-proof water bowl of his own design in the bottom of the car.

As he kicked life into the motor, the deep rumble put a smile on his face. He strapped on his helmet, and they rolled out toward the old highway after dropping the house key off to Jimmy.

Pretty soon, Gracie was in her element, ears flapping in the wind, tongue slobbering on the side of her face, bearing that famous Golden grin.

A family in a minivan pulled up beside them at their next stop and three little girls started waving and smiling. It was just like Gracie to make strangers smile everywhere she went.

Just for fun, Calvin put a special horn on the sidecar just for Gracie: a bark. He hit the "bark" button and the kids went crazy with giggles. Their parents finally pulled away and Calvin gave them the traditional biker wave.

About an hour or so later, he pulled into the town of Slickrock. There was something big going on by the look of traffic, banners, and people everywhere. As they cruised down Main Street, he saw a banner over the bridge: "50th Annual Slickrock Bike Show and Rally."

He had heard a lot about this event and for some reason or another, he was never able to go. It was $10 to get in and $30 for a show booth.

"Ya know, Gracie, I think we should enter the show, I have a good feeling about this."

He paid the fee and made his way to his assigned spot. He took Gracie out to stretch and hit the adjacent dog park so she could take care of business.

He wasn't really prepared for the show in a way that he would have liked. He also wasn't going to pass this up.

He recalled something his grandpa used to tell him all the time: "When opportunity presents itself, be open enough to explore it. It may not be for you, but you won't know until you go through that door." So, he wiped his bike down with a microfiber towel that he kept in a saddle bag and he left a few of his art creation business cards on the windscreen. He grabbed Gracie's leash and they set out to check out the other motorbikes.

Two hot dogs from a food truck later, they got back to his bike. There were a few people crowded around it, checking it out. One couple, in matching bike leathers, got his attention.

"Hi, this is your bike? It's really cool."

"Thanks."

The couple continued, "We have been looking forever for a sidecar like this to fit on our old Harley. Where did you get this?"

"Like you, I looked forever but never saw anything that I really liked. I bought a few and tossed 'em after a while, because they didn't quite do the trick, so I just decided to make my own."

"Well, you did a great job, because this looks like a pro did it," the male of the couple said with a smile. The biker's wife was really checking out Gracie's sidecar. She had a big smile on her face. She was imagining her own puppy finally being able to go for a ride with them.

Calvin continued describing how he came up with his design. "I came up with this after a lot of trial and error runs. The sidecar has its own suspension, which smooths out the ride for Gracie. The floor is extra cushy, and the material is non-slip, so she has something to grip to. There is even a spill-proof water dish for her."

The biker's wife spoke up, "We have been looking for a long time. Do you think you could make one of these for us?"

Calvin scratched the back of his head for a moment as he pondered the idea. Doing this for money had never occurred to him until now. Selling his other "creations" was something he did on the side, but he'd never had a custom order.

"You know, I hadn't really ever figured on doing this for anyone else, but it might be a fun project to see if I can duplicate it. I think we should give it a whirl." He stuck out his hand to shake the biker's hand. They traded contact information and set up a meeting for the next week.

He took a blanket out of the side pod and spread it on the ground. It wasn't long before another couple walked up. They seemed to already know Gracie.

"Oh, my God, it's Goggle Dog!" Of course, Gracie was up in a moment, tail wagging, ready to make some new friends. "Do you mind if we pet her?"

Calvin laughed and said it would be okay. "Goggle Dog? Where did you get that from?"

"Oh, you haven't seen the video yet? You are trending on the Internet right now. I guess some young girls saw you on the freeway and took a video of you waving at them."

Calvin pictured the girls in the minivan and smiled.

"Oh, one of three girls in a minivan must've took it and posted it online. They were really excited to see Gracie with goggles on. I have a horn on the bike that sounds like a bark. They really got a kick out of that!" Calvin reached down and triggered the bark horn. Everyone laughed when they heard it.

Calvin continued, "I can't believe I'm on the Internet. It's been a crazy rollercoaster ride for me this week, but it's shaping up to be a fantastic weekend—way better than I would have ever figured."

He grinned, a bit honored that Gracie was becoming a star.

"Where did you get your sidecar? We have been looking for one for our Golden, too."

"Well, like I just told another couple, I couldn't find anything that I really liked that would work with my vintage bike. So, I made one with all the stuff I thought was important to me and Gracie."

"Do you think you could make one for us? We would love to be able to take our dogs for a ride, too."

"Well, I am open to talking about it and see what we can do. Here's my card. Give me a call next week and we can set something up. Email me the details about the type of bike that you have, too. That will help a lot."

Calvin sat down on his blanket and Gracie curled up next to him. His head was spinning with all of the things that had happened this weekend that he still hadn't really sorted out.

After the show was over, like many of the other folks, he headed down to a popular local diner. It was special because they allowed dogs on the patio.

Calvin was halfway through his dinner when Carrie, the owner, came by to greet them and meet Gracie. She had a special place in her heart for dogs, which is why she allowed them on the patio.

"Hi, I'm Carrie. This is my diner. Are they taking good care of you? And who is this pretty girl with you?"

Calvin stood up to shake her hand. "Hi, I'm Calvin. This is Gracie. She just turned eight years old."

Carrie looked at them with a smile, "I kinda knew this was Gracie. Everyone has been talking about your video online. A few of my regulars showed me because they knew I would think it's cute. I didn't expect to see you in my diner, though. You two are famous and are so cute together!"

"I actually had nothing to do with that. It was a complete surprise to me. One of three girls we saw in a minivan at a stop next to us took it and posted it. I will have to figure out how I can send those girls a thank-you note. It was a really nice thing they did."

"That's pretty easy. I can show you how if you want. Where are y'all staying tonight?"

Calvin threw up his hands and a grimace crossed his face. "I have no idea. I'm pretty sure that everything is booked up. We didn't plan on being here. We'll probably just cowboy camp in the park next to the bike. It should be a nice night for it."

Cassie's eyes flew wide open. "What? There is no way I am going to let you sleep in the park with that precious dog! Don't leave before we have a chance to talk more. I have to take care of a few things but I will be right back." She waved over his server. "Gretchen, will you get him some more coffee and bring him some apple cobbler, too? And bring the broken pie crust pieces we save for the good puppies."

"Okay, sure."

Not knowing what she had on her mind, Calvin agreed to stick around.

For some reason that he couldn't explain, the tiny voice in his gut said to stay put. Gracie didn't growl at her, and dogs are a really good judge of character. So, he waited for her to return.

A short while later, Cassie came back and sat on the other side of his booth.

"I realize that we don't really know each other, given that we just met today. But the thought of you and Gracie sleeping in the park really bothers me. I have a casita that is empty right now and I would love for you to be my guests this weekend. You can stay as long as you'd like."

"You're not worried about a stranger staying at your place?" Calvin queried.

"Look, I have seen a lot of people in this line of work, and figure I am a pretty good judge of character. Plus, you have a Golden. You can't be a bad guy and have a cool dog like Gracie. I'm sure everything will be just fine."

Calvin wasn't sure what to say for a moment. He looked down at Gracie, who was eagerly looking back up at him.

Her tail wagged and she gave him a lick. That seemed to settle that question pretty quickly.

"Wow, that's very kind of you, and yes, we would be happy to be your guests. Thank you. I am sure that Gracie was not looking forward to sleeping on the blanket all night."

"You're welcome. Here are the keys and directions. Go ahead and make yourselves at home. I'll probably see you in the morning."

Calvin loaded up Gracie in the side car then headed for the house. The well-kept white bungalow with bright blue trim and a matching front door greeted them as they pulled into the driveway. Almost like a cliché, a wraparound porch, complete with a rope swing, completed the picture. It was perfect for relaxing with a drink after a long day. Behind the main house was the casita with the same paint scheme.

"Gracie, I think we have hit the jackpot this weekend. This is better than any hotel room in town, and Cassie is beautiful and nice, too. What do you think?" Gracie wagged her tail and let out a short bark.

The inside was arranged like a one-bedroom apartment. It was quaint and well-appointed with stainless-steel kitchen appliances. The bathroom had a nice shower. There was even a special spot for visiting dogs with a comfy bed, as well as water and food bowls with paw-print designs on them in the kitchen.

Calvin took a shower, found a couple of beers in the refrigerator, and then settled down on the couch. He began thinking about making sidecars for a living—or, at least, as a side hustle. He loved teaching, but he also loved making things. There was a lot to think about. He was smart enough to realize that making custom pieces might be a profitable niche business. Because of his grandpa's advice, he was never one to dismiss an opportunity. It deserved some serious thought.

Calvin climbed into bed after putting his beer bottle away. He didn't want Cassie to think he was a slob. The bed was perfect, and he slept until morning.

He woke up to the smell of coffee and bacon and followed the aromas to the back door of the main house where the kitchen was.

"Good morning, sleepyhead. It's about time you woke up," Cassie joked. She handed him a mug. "How do you take your coffee?"

"Good morning to you, too. Something smells really good. I like it hot, blonde, and sweet."

Cassie laughed. For as long as she had been in the restaurant biz, only the old-schoolers referred to that expression for cream and sugar. She wondered if he got that expression from his father or grandfather.

Just as Calvin and Cassie sat down in the kitchen, Gracie came strolling across the yard with something hanging from just one tooth. As she bounded up the steps, Calvin started laughing.

Cassie looked at them both with a quizzical look on her face. "What on earth does she have hanging from her mouth?"

Calvin looked at his puppy and sighed. "Gracie, even here? Have you no shame?"

Just like at home, Gracie was carrying one of Calvin's socks around, hanging precariously from just one tooth, as always. She plopped onto the couch with the sock between her paws and wagged her tail, thumping it against the back cushion. Calvin began his explanation.

"This started about six months ago. I had been looking for my flannel pajama bottoms. They weren't on the bed, as they usually were, nor were they in the hamper or even the bathroom. I didn't think much about it and grabbed another pair and went to bed.

The same thing happened the next day. I came home from work, sat on the couch with a beer, and saw both my bottoms. They were right there, with Gracie on top of them, looking as proud as can be.

"At first, I was thinking she was going to eat them or shred them. I got after her and later, I realized that she was just hanging on to them like they were a security blanket of sorts. Then she started doing the same with my socks. Now, it's just funny and sometimes annoying that I have to look in the living room for my pajamas or socks, instead of my room. What's really funny is how she manages to hook my sock around her tooth!"

Carrie was laughing so hard at this point that a few tears started running down her face. She put her coffee down and went over to Gracie. Of course, Gracie was wagging her tail harder now. She got a great big hug from Cassie, who was rewarded with a big lick on her nose.

"That is just about the cutest thing I have ever heard. She clearly loves her papa." She looked at Calvin with a twinkle in her eye.

Calvin looked at her sideways now. "What's that look for?"

"Oh, nothing. So, how did you end up in Slickrock? Where is your wife?" Calvin nearly swallowed his coffee the wrong way. He was not expecting that question.

"Oh, the direct approach! I like that. I'm all about that, too. A fair question, it is." A pained look came across his face and disappeared as quickly as it appeared—but not before she noticed it.

"Oh, no, I'm sorry if I brought up something I wasn't supposed to." Cassie turned red with embarrassment.

Calvin told her of the story of how he landed here in town.

Cassie sat across from him with a sad look on her face.

"I am so sorry. Some women can be so mean. I don't understand why. She had nothing to gain from it. However, I believe in karma, and someday, somehow, she will get hers. It would be fun to be there when it happens," she said with a mock evil laugh.

Calvin laughed so hard he just about spit out his coffee. "I knew I liked you for a reason! Maybe one day, I will have to thank her. If she hadn't done that, God only knows where I would be right now. I'm sure I would not be having this fantastic weekend, nor would I have met you."

"So, you are a glass-half-full kinda guy?"

"Yeah, I suppose that I am. Looking at it any other way doesn't accomplish much. I'm real, and serious about the things that I need to be. Other than that, I'm pretty easy-breezy. Now, it's your turn. How did you end up here?"

"Well, I will give you the short version of it. Many years ago, I had my first job in a coffee place down in Phoenix called The Coffee Stand. I was only sixteen years old."

"Really? The Coffee Stand? The one in the Valley?

"Yeah, why?"

"Everyone knows about The Coffee Stand. It's an institution. Been there forever. Shoot, I probably saw you there and never even knew it. We still go there. My buddy, Jimmy, and I meet there all the time."

"Well, back then, the owners took a liking to me and started teaching me how to cook and bake. Thanks to them, I fell in love with the food business, and I have been doing it ever since.

"About five years ago, this place came up for sale and the owners of The Coffee Stand fronted me some money to buy it. Before this, I was a partner in a boutique café in Boulder. It was going well for a while, until I found out that my partner was skimming money. He ran off to Mexico, and I had to sell everything to make it right to my vendors and employees. It still leaves a bad taste in my mouth, even though it's been a while."

"Wow. That is fantastic. It looks like you have been making a good go of it, too."

"Thank you. It's been a lot of fun."

Carrie got up to refill her cup. She topped off Calvin's at the same time.

"So, there is talk amongst the group that you might be looking into building sidecars for some people. Is that true?"

Calvin put down his coffee mug and shook his head in disbelief. "I have no idea how so many people are talking about that. I have only spoken with two people and said we can bat some ideas around. I haven't committed to build anything yet. I haven't had a chance to fully explore the idea myself, let alone have people spreading word about it."

"Well, tell me what you have so far."

"Cassie, I know that I have just barely met you. When it comes to this stuff, I am very straightforward and don't beat around the bush. What are you getting at?"

"You know, you are cute when you get serious," she said with a smile.

The grimace remained on his face. Cassie took the hint.

"Oh, you *weren't* joking, were you?"

Calvin sighed and shook his head.

Cassie continued, "I think you could be on to something special. Here you have a sidecar built for dogs—or cats, for that matter. No one else is building those. In less than forty-eight hours, you and Gracie have trended on the Internet because of what you built, and you've had two different people express serious interest in having you build one for them, too. If that's not enough to prove interest in the concept, I don't know what is. I know an opportunity when I see it, and this is it. Have you thought about how you will fund it?"

"Shoot, I haven't even figured on it being a business till a few hours ago. So, no."

"There is a thing now called crowdsourcing. You put up a business plan on their site and if people are interested, they can invest a small amount. If enough people invest, you get the money."

Calvin picked up his coffee and took a long draw off it, then said, "I want to thank you for letting me stay here last night and taking a chance on a stranger. You are a fantastic person, and this will not be forgotten anytime soon. Can we talk next week, after I have a chance to digest all this?"

"Oh, of course," Cassie agreed with a smile.

So, Calvin packed up, loaded Gracie in the bike, and they headed for home. He wanted to get on the road before all of the crazy going-home traffic started.

Once home, he bathed Gracie because she was dirty from all the outdoors stuff, then he took a shower and started the laundry. He still had to show up for his regular job on Monday. Teaching wasn't really his life's calling, but he was good at it and it paid pretty well. It was not an easy thing to just walk away from just yet.

* * * * *

After a month, the Cat Project, as Jimmy and Lauren had come to call it, was finally done. Jimmy could not believe how much fun he had with it. Not admitting to anyone but himself yet, he liked working side by side with Lauren, too. She wasn't there for all of the project, but she visited regularly to see how it was going.

Of course, Mrs. Marsh made a big to-do out of it all. The moment it was completed, she invited many of her friends over for tea, to check out her newest home project. As Jimmy and Lauren showed the guests around, telling them all about the project, several of them asked for Jimmy's card for some future work.

* * * * *

When the following Friday arrived, Calvin called Jimmy to have a beer at the pub.

Calvin said he had a young lady in mind to be Jimmy's helper. She had been a star student in all of the vocational classes, and showed a knack for picking things up quickly and knowing how to fix them the right way. She had just graduated.

She also needed the money to help support her family.

He also told Jimmy about his three-day ride and all that had happened. Jimmy could not have been more excited for his best friend.

They were still catching up when someone at the bar caught Calvin's eye. It was a young man who seemed a little out of place. He was a bit overdressed for the cowboy bar. His khaki pants and polo shirt stuck out amongst the blue jeans and boots worn by most of the pub's patrons.

"Hey, Jimmy, check out the guy at the end of the bar." Calvin poked Jimmy on the shoulder.

"Why, what's up?"

"I have a feeling he's about to get shot down by the blonde a few chairs down from him. I think he's going to try and buy her a drink."

Jimmy grimaced.

"Oh, crap, that isn't going to be pretty. I remember when we tried that for a whole summer."

Calvin laughed at the painful memory.

"Damn. Don't remind me. TV and the movies sure lied to us about how it easy it was to pick up girls at bars. I still have the scars!"

The preppy young man got the attention of the bartender.

"Hi, what can I get for you?" she asked.

"What's that lady at the end drinking? I'd like to buy her a round." It was hard to miss the nervousness in his voice.

"I'll take care of that for you."

She made the drink and placed it in front of the young lady with some nodding and finger-pointing as to who it came from. The young man waved and gave a shy smile. The young lady smiled then shook her head and hand to say, "No thanks."

She got up from her chair, left the drink on the bar, and went in the direction of some people on the other side of the pub. Jimmy, Calvin, and the bartender saw the sad look on his face as he tried to crawl into an imaginary black hole.

Jimmy spoke up. "That was brutal."

They could hear the bartender talking to the devastated young man. "I'm sorry about that."

The young man just stood up and trudged out a side door.

Jimmy looked at Calvin. "That is why we quit asking out girls. We didn't stand a chance with our goofy looks and not-so-cool clothes. I am still wary about asking a girl out on a date."

They turned their attention back to business and catching up.

* * * * *

They set up an interview with Jimmy's prospective helper for the next day. Cecilia—or Cici, as she liked to be called—was seventeen, nice, seemed to know her stuff, and could work full-time. Most importantly, she had her driver's license and a good driving record. He hired her right on the spot. She would start Monday morning.

Later that night, while they were having dinner, Papa Joe asked, "How are things going in the Lauren department?"

"Dad, I really like her. She was really fun to work with on the Cat Project. We laughed a lot and got the job done, too. She is really smart and knows her way around a house, for sure." He also told his dad about the young man at the pub. Papa Joe just shook his head.

"Son, girls haven't changed at all. They used to do that to us poor sailors on leave, too. Speaking of picking up girls, are you ever going to ask Lauren out on a real date? Also, when do I get to meet her? You know your mom would have already met her and they would be best friends."

They both laughed as they remembered how his mom had been.

Jimmy didn't have an answer for his father.

* * * * *

Hey, Mom,

I sure wish you were here for this. I need some girl advice and Dad is not as good at this stuff as you were. I am sure you would like Lauren, if you met her. You know, the last time I moved too fast with a girl, it blew up badly. I don't have time for that now. I hope you can help me do it right this time. I know we have only known each other for a short time, but something just feels right about her and I can't shake it.

Chapter 8: Finally, Papa Joe

Later the next week, Lauren called Jimmy.

"Hey, Jimmy, I've been thinking about changing all my lights to LED, but I hate messing with electricity. Can you come by and take a look?"

"Hey, Lauren, I was meaning to call you and say hi. Great minds think alike." He giggled at his own joke, while he could swear that he heard eyeballs roll from the other side of the phone.

"Yeah, I can come by this afternoon, if you like. What's a good time?"

"Why don't you make it four-thirty? I should be done with my client meetings by then."

"Sounds good. See ya then."

Jimmy had other jobs that day. He got through them as quickly as possible so he could go home, shower, and clean up before he went to Lauren's.

Of course, Papa Joe saw what was going on and laughed.

"Son, you must really like her if you're going to this kind of trouble for her. So, when am I going to meet her?"

"Dad, I hope more sooner than later. I have a funny feeling about this one today. She knows full well how to change out bulbs for LED lights."

"Well, Jimmy, if that's the case, you'd better bring that bottle of red wine that's in the rack. Ya know, just in case." Papa Joe winked at him. Under his breath, half-talking to himself, he added, "Ooh, I have a good feeling about this."

"Dad! I heard that!"

"Heard what? I have no idea what you are going on about. Don't make that lady wait for you now."

Jimmy knew his dad was right. In this case, it was better to have the bottle and not need it than the other way around. He checked his watch, dusted off the bottle, and headed for his truck. He stowed the bottle in a safe place, nestled amid a work rag, so it wouldn't break.

When he arrived at Lauren's, he knocked on her door, which she immediately opened.

Lauren noticed right away that he was a little cleaner than he normally was at the end of a day.

She looked at him with a wry smile and a twinkle in her eyes. "Did you go home and clean up before you came over here?"

Jimmy got a little shy and avoided eye contact with her right away. He was hoping she wouldn't notice quite so quickly.

"Well," he said quickly trying to cover himself, "I had a particularly stinky job just before yours and I didn't want to bring that into your house."

He smiled his big smile at her and batted his eyes just for fun.

"Hmmm, sho 'nuf," Lauren drawled in her best southern accent. She then led him into the hallway, and it didn't take long for him to switch out the lights. He also couldn't help smelling the chicken and potatoes roasting in the oven. He hoped that she didn't hear his tummy rumbling.

"Hey, that smells really good. Whatcha cooking?" Jimmy declared as he walked back into the kitchen.

"Oh, I am making chicken and potatoes with carrots."

Jimmy wrinkled his nose at the thought of carrots. Lauren caught that and laughed.

"You don't like carrots? What on earth is wrong with you? Everyone likes carrots!"

"Nope, not this boy. Ironically enough, carrot cake is my favorite cake."

"Well, you can pick them out of your bowl—that is if you care to stay for dinner?"

Jimmy's eyes lit up. He was more than happy to eat with her. Both he and his dad were pretty good in the kitchen, but he never turned down a home-cooked meal made by someone else.

"Let me put my tools away. I might have something that will go well with this."

He sped out the kitchen door before she had a chance to ask what it was.

When he walked back into the kitchen with the bottle, she started laughing. "You had that all along, didn't you? It looks like someone was hoping he could stay for dinner."

He set the bottle on the table and grinned while holding an imaginary halo over his head. "What? Me? No way. A client of mine gave this to me, and it's just been riding around in the truck with me all day. Let me call my dad and tell him I'll be late making dinner."

"There will be plenty here. You should take him some."

"He doesn't even know you yet, and he's gonna be in love. Chicken and potatoes, sans carrots, is his favorite dish."

Lauren busied herself with taking the roast pan out of the oven and setting the table for two while Jimmy stepped into the next room to make his call.

After they started eating, Lauren suddenly put down her fork and looked straight at him.

"When am I going to meet your dad, by the way? I am really curious now, from all the stories you tell of him."

"You wanna meet him? Really?"

Jimmy had a puzzled look on his face. "Not that there has been a lot of them, but I never met the parents of my past girlfriends. I thought that was something you do after you got engaged or something. Mind you, my relationships with those girls weren't anything really serious because they happened during my mid-teenage years. And my last two were both a sandwich short of a picnic."

He laughed at the memory.

Lauren just smiled at his joke.

Jimmy took another bite of chicken before he answered.

"Well, funny thing is, he was wondering when he was gonna meet you too."

"So, what did you say?" Lauren's face started to turn more serious than it was a few moments ago

"I didn't say anything, but I guess we can arrange something soon. Let me talk to my Dad and see what he has going on."

Although he knew that this topic would come up eventually with Lauren, he wasn't prepared for it tonight.

After dinner, the two continued to talk and drink.

After the wine came some coffee. Jimmy didn't want to drive while feeling the effects of the wine, so he didn't get home until about ten o'clock.

The next morning, Papa Joe rolled into the kitchen. Jimmy was whistling a tune while he made breakfast.

The coffee pot was already full. Papa Joe poured himself a cup and said, "Hey there, Romeo, what time did you get in last night? Looks like someone woke up on the right side of the bed this morning. What's going on, son?"

"We were eating dinner and she asked why she hasn't met you yet. She's heard all the stories and is very curious about you. I couldn't think of a way to wiggle out of that question. And I didn't want to introduce y'all, because you're gonna like her as much as I do."

Papa Joe had a big smile on his face. He could not have been happier knowing that his only son was finally truly in love with someone and she was in love with him back.

"So, when do I get to meet this young lady?"

"Would Sunday for dinner be too soon?"

"Jimmy, I can't think of a better day. I am looking forward to telling her all of the 'young Jimmy' stories I can remember." Papa Joe laughed out loud like he hadn't had a good belly laugh in quite some time.

Jimmy rolled his eyes at his dad, hoping he was joking and wouldn't embarrass him, then picked up his phone to text Lauren.

'Dad wants to meet you. How about Sunday at 2 p.m.?'

'Perfect!'

Later that night, with a glass of scotch on his desk, Jimmy reached for his journal.

> *Dear Mom,*
>
> *Wow, I'm excited. It's finally going to happen. Lauren's gonna meet Dad. I told her about him and the wheelchair. I didn't want to surprise her with that and then have her bolt. She said she is looking forward to meeting him. The other girls never said that. We may really be on to something here.*

Chapter 9: The Bridge

Calvin had been home for a few days and had started testing a new sidecar design. He noticed that Gracie seemed a lot more tired than normal. She was not the young pup that she had been when he got her six years ago. He figured that all the excitement from the weekend had caught up with her and she was just recovering a little slower now. She refused to eat. She barely went outside to do her business. A few more days passed and there was no improvement. When she refused to get out of bed, Calvin rushed Gracie to the vet.

He had been to quite a few veterinarians in his time, and of them all, Dr. Rachel was his favorite. Something just clicked with her and her staff, and of course, they loved Gracie. Besides being kind to her patients, she also never baby-talked to them. Calvin hated that and never did it with Gracie.

The whole staff was worried as Calvin carried Gracie into the clinic. They got her into an exam room right away. The vet tech, Kara, came in, and took Gracie's vitals. Shortly after that, Dr. Rachel came in. Gracie slowly wagged her tail when she saw her favorite vet. Calvin told her what he had noticed while she looked Gracie over. Dr. Rachel took her back to the lab to get X-rays and bloodwork. Calvin sat in the little exam room for close to an hour, alternating between nervously playing with his phone and trying to read the dog magazines that were on the side table. He was worried about his dog and couldn't really concentrate on anything else.

The pit in his stomach grew.

Finally, he heard a soft knock.

Dr. Rachel came back in with Gracie, who was barely wagging her tail now. She looked really tired and stressed.

Somehow, Calvin knew the news wasn't going to be good.

"Calvin, we have done the X-rays and bloodwork, and it seems that Gracie has an advanced stage of cancer. Like most dogs, she did a very good job of hiding it from all of us. Unfortunately, it's too advanced for treatment. The best thing to take away her pain is to put her down. I know this is not the news you were hoping for, but if you don't want Gracie to continue suffering, it's the most humane thing we can do. So, what are your wishes as to where we go from here?"

Tears streamed down Calvin's face. This was what he had feared but not wanted to face just yet. Things were going so well in his life right now and this was a kick in the gut. He looked into Gracie's eyes and held her head in his hands.

Gracie looked back at him as if to say, "I'm really sick and I hung in there as long as I could so you didn't have to worry too much. You have been a great dad, the best a dog could ever ask for. You know what to do. Don't drag it out any longer than you need to."

Dr. Rachel and Cindy had tears in their eyes, too. Gracie was one of their first and favorite patients.

"Doc, go ahead and put her to sleep. She has been a fine dog—the best ever. I don't want her to suffer any more. She deserves to die with dignity."

The vet left the room and came back in a few minutes with what she needed. As she prepped Gracie for her injection, she talked to Calvin.

"You are more than welcome to stay as long as you need to say goodbye. Do you want us to take care of her when you leave?"

Calvin nodded.

The vet put Gracie upon a blanket on top of the exam table. Calvin cradled Gracie as her last shot was injected. She closed her eyes for the last time. The vet confirmed that she had crossed over and quietly left the room.

Calvin held her paw and stroked her fur. With tears streaming down his face, he talked to her for about an hour, telling her stories he remembered from when she was a puppy and all the trouble she had gotten into.

There was one night when he stayed out too late, and she got into a bag of flour. She had the time of her life as she dragged flour all over the house. There were little dough balls all over her lips after she got a drink of water.

He half-laughed and half-cried at the memory.

Eventually, he said his final goodbye and left, using the side door.

When he got home, he sat on the couch with a glass of scotch. He toasted her and went to bed. "Gracie, you have been the love of my life. I am going to miss you always."

When he got up in the morning, it felt oddly quiet in the house. Usually, Gracie would wake him up with a lick.

He made some coffee and was still numb from her sudden passing. He knew he would have to put her things away soon but couldn't bring himself to do it just yet.

A text message came across his phone from Cassie, the lovely lady who let him and Gracie stay in her casita.

'Just checking in with you and Gracie. I hope y'all are okay. Call whenever you want to.'

He texted her back right away.

'Hi, I'm not good. I just had to put Gracie down due to cancer. I will call you later today, I promise.'

'I understand, I will be waiting for you.'

Calvin finished his coffee and went to clean up and get dressed.

While he was in the shower, he decided that he needed some wind therapy to help him heal.

He packed some clothes in a day bag, and soon, it was time to hit the highway again. This time, he left the sidecar in the garage and took his BMW touring bike.

He didn't have a route in mind, just wherever the wind blew him.

Without thinking about it, he ended up taking the scenic route to Slickrock.

He found Cassie's diner and was soon in a familiar seat. Cassie came out with two cups of coffee and some apple pie.

She gave him a hug and then sat right next to him.

"I'm really sorry about Gracie. Are you okay?"

Calvin took a long sip of coffee and swallowed before he answered.

"Yeah. No. I don't know. It was pretty rough yesterday, but I know she is in a better place now. The house is just so quiet without her running around. It's a little hard to stay there right now, so I had to go for a ride. The bike just sort of found its way here."

"Sweetie, I totally get it, and you are welcome to stay here as long as you would like." Cassie put her hand on his shoulder and rubbed it comfortingly. She added, "Actually, I can have Lou cover for me, and we could go for a ride, if you want to."

Calvin's eyes lit up.

He knew that she rode because he had seen a bike in her garage when he stayed with her the last time he was there.

"I would love that very much! When do you wanna go?"

With a twinkle in her eye and a little pep in her step, she smiled and said, "Let me go get changed, and we can head right out. Meet me at my house."

A little while later, she came out of her garage wearing full leathers. Like Calvin, she could not understand how some riders did not wear protective gear. All it would take would be a bug hitting you in the face at 70 miles per hour in the wrong spot and a nasty—if not fatal—wreck could ensue.

Cassie took the lead and they headed toward a scenic canyon road with enough twists and turns to satisfy even the most eager canyon riders. At the end of the road was a small lake and marina.

Surprisingly, they had the lake almost to themselves. As they walked along the lake path talking about everything and nothing, Calvin instinctively put his hand out to hold hers. She took his hand, and looked at him with her eyes as if to say, "Wow, this is nice," and squeezed his hand a little more.

His heart skipped a beat and then began beating a mile a minute while his mind tried to tell him that this was really happening—sparks were flying.

They stopped to watch a bald eagle fly in low lazy circles over the lake until he suddenly tucked in his wings with the utmost grace and swooped down, crashing into the water. He came out with a large fish wiggling at the end of his sharp talons and flew off to feed his family.

Cassie turned to face Calvin, still holding his hand.

He took the other one in his hand and pulled her closer. Their eyes locked and he kissed her ever so softly on the lips. She pulled him in even closer and kissed him back.

"Cassie?"

"Yes?"

"I am not as good as some other guys in the 'smooth lines' department, so I will just tell you straight. I like you a lot and would like to see where this takes us, if that's okay with you. I'd also like to add that you are a wonderful kisser."

She laughed and turned a couple of shades of red.

"Calvin, I really like you, and would also love to see where this goes. For the record, you are a great kisser, too."

Now, it was Calvin's turn to blush. A goofy smile came across his face that expressed everything he was feeling now.

Cassie brought him back to reality.

"Hey, it's getting a little dark out, and we should be heading back. Besides, I'm getting hungry."

With that, they climbed back on their bikes and headed back up the road in a cloud of dust.

Chapter 10: Dinner with Papa Joe

Sunday morning came around a little faster than Jimmy figured. The kitchen was a blur of activity as Jimmy and Papa Joe got everything ready. Jimmy wanted to put on a good meal for Lauren's first official visit.

Lauren kept asking throughout the week what could she bring.

Jimmy said, "Nothing, just bring yourself."

Well, that wasn't the way she was raised, so she knew she would at least bring something.

Lauren knew Papa Joe liked a good scotch, so she made sure to pick out a nice one from the liquor store in town where she knew the owner. She had just redesigned his home. He helped her with the selection.

Jimmy sometimes insisted that he wasn't a great cook, but when it mattered, he could put together a helluva spread. Tonight's dinner was smoked brisket, garlic mashed potatoes, broccoli, and two small carrots just for Lauren. There was pecan pie with vanilla ice cream for dessert.

It was about two that afternoon when Lauren knocked, announcing her arrival.

As Jimmy opened the door, the amazing aromas of foods cooking in the kitchen wafted out.

Lauren took a good sniff and smiled at Jimmy. "I thought you said you couldn't cook!"

"Oh, no, I said I'm not a chef, although I haven't done too badly in that department. I'm certainly not the skinny high school kid I used to be!" Jimmy laughed as he patted his not-so-skinny tummy.

Just then, Papa Joe rolled into the kitchen with a big smile on his face.

"You must be the redhead he keeps telling me about."

"D-a-d, stop! I never said it like that." Jimmy laughingly objected to that slight.

Lauren came over, bent down, and gave Papa Joe a giant hug.

"Papa Joe, I am so happy to meet you. Jimmy won't stop talking about you when we are out on jobs together." She handed him the bottle of scotch.

Jimmy was still objecting, "Oh, what, you too? Ganging up on the kid, I see!"

Papa Joe just couldn't resist the opening. "Son, you had better stop complaining, or I will tell her about your high school adventures!"

Lauren's ears and eyes perked up over that one. "Ooh, these I have to hear. He is always telling me he was a good kid and never got in trouble."

"Hmmm, it seems that two can play this game. I got stories about Dad, too, so it's gonna be a long afternoon."

"Then it's a good thing I brought the good stuff for Papa Joe," Lauren quipped.

Looking around, she asked, "Jimmy, what can I do to help?"

"Thank you, but there is nothing really left to do. Have a drink and just relax in the living room. I'll call you when dinner is ready."

They poured drinks and Papa Joe rolled out of the kitchen. "Follow me."

Lauren carried their beverages and made herself comfortable on the sofa. A little while later, Jimmy announced that dinner was ready. They gathered around the table. When Jimmy put a plate in front of her, she started laughing. "Aww, you made two little carrots just for me."

Dinner went off well with lots of embarrassing stories about Jimmy. While Papa Joe tried to rope Lauren into a story or two, she skillfully wriggled out of them.

She winked at him and declared, "Papa Joe, a girl can't tell you everything on the first date, you know."

That made Jimmy and Lauren laugh. Papa Joe seemed to turn red and shy for a moment—certainly a first for him in quite some time.

* * * * *

Hi, Mom,
Dinner with the three of us went well.
Dad and Lauren totally hit it off with each
other. Mom, I am sure you would have really
liked her. Now, if I can just not screw it up by
being me. I'll be okay, I think… right?

* * * * *

A few days later, a hand-addressed letter came for Papa Joe in the mail. The penmanship looked like it was from a woman, and since he didn't know very many at his age, he ripped it right open.

It was a card from Lauren thanking him for the wonderful dinner. Jimmy saw him reading the card.

"Hey Dad, you got a card from someone? Who from? What does it say?"

Papa Joe could not resist the opportunity to rib his unwitting son, especially when it was this easy. He kept a straight face while he explained it to Jimmy.

"It's a love letter from your ex-girlfriend, Lauren. She says she wants to go steady with me now."

"WHAT?" Jimmy ran over and about and snatched the card right out of his dad's hands. He pulled his glasses out and paused a moment to read the note. When he was done, he shook his head and rolled his eyes. Before both of them started laughing, Jimmy looked at his dad and claimed, "You suck!"

"Son, you had better not let go of this girl. She is amazing, and the fact that she likes hanging out with you and me—she's gotta be the one."

"I know, Dad. That thought has been growing in my mind for some time now. I am not sure what I did to deserve her, but I feel pretty lucky. I didn't quite want to admit it, but it seems you two like each other a lot, and that just made it more real now."

Chapter 11: The Ladder Crash

The following Monday morning, Jimmy knew that he and Cici were going to have a full week. It had been going really well with Cici. She had been with him for a couple of weeks and was coming along in her skills. The reports he got from his customers were fantastic. They all liked her.

His job that morning was not one that he was looking forward to and it was something that only he would let himself do. He had to replace some of the burnt-out light bulbs in a home that had 20-foot tall, vaulted ceilings. Mrs. Otterminder, the sweet old lady whom he helped before, had no business climbing a ladder of any height. Jimmy was going to be alone in the house all day because she was working one of her occasional nursing shifts.

He was happy that he had an inside job today because it was raining quite heavily. He carried in his long ladder and did his best to dry it off before he made a mess everywhere. After silently thanking the builder for putting the breaker box in the garage, Jimmy shut off the power to the living room.

He then got to work.

Satisfied that his ladder was secure and steady, he started up the rungs with one hand on the ladder side and two light bulbs in the other hand. Lightning flashed, and the stillness in the house was broken by a huge clap of thunder.

To make things worse, his phone vibrated in his pocket at the exact same time. Startled, his foot slipped off the rung. As much as he tried to hang on, he slid down the ladder, hit the couch, and then bounced onto the tile floor. The ladder went the other way and crashed through the dining room table.

Searing pain shot through his shoulder and left arm. He screamed out and at the same time realized that no one could hear him. Mrs. Otterminder was at the hospital.

Laying on the tile floor, trying to catch his breath and move as little as possible, he looked himself over as well as he could.

He was grateful he didn't see or feel any blood.

He spotted his phone halfway across the tiled floor. He took a deep a breath and began inching himself across the tiles. Keeping his injured arm stable while reaching for his phone with the good arm was another experience in pain.

He opened his phone and hit the 911 emergency button. The operator said she would stay on the phone with him until the paramedics arrived, and she talked him through some breathing and meditation exercises to help minimize the pain in his shoulder.

When the EMTs arrived ten minutes later, they gave him a shot to reduce the pain and then loaded him in the ambulance. The paramedics said they would lock up the house when they left and leave the keys in the mailbox. En route to the hospital, he also asked them to call Lauren to let her know what had happened.

She raced to the hospital and got there in time to see him just before they wheeled him into the X-ray department. He was dazed and loopy from the drugs and it took him a minute to realize it was Lauren leaning over him.

"Hi, babe." Jimmy had a goofy look on his face and his speech was slurred. "What are you here for? Did you break something too?" He sounded like that one night he'd had five margaritas. He was a happy drunk and she was thankful for that. She laughed at how cute he was.

"Oh, sweetie, I am glad you are okay."

The nurse came to wheel him down the hall.

"Guess I gotta go now. Whee!" Jimmy said as he disappeared behind the swinging doors.

Lauren hated waiting rooms and decided to wait in the cafeteria until the doctors called her back upstairs.

Jimmy was still a little loopy when they wheeled him into the discharge lobby along with his belongings. Before she left, she called Papa Joe to let them know what had happened and they were coming home soon.

Once they got Jimmy settled into a recliner chair that was going to be his home for the next couple of days, Lauren gave him some more painkillers and he was out for the night. She then called Cici and instructed her to retrieve the keys from Mrs. Otterminder's mailbox and clean up whatever mess was there.

Lauren was still at the house in the morning when Papa Joe wheeled into the kitchen to make coffee. She had slept on the couch next to Jimmy to keep an eye on him.

"Good morning, young lady. He's a tough kid. He will be alright. I'm about to make some coffee. Would you like some?"

"Oh, Papa Joe, I didn't hear you roll in. How are you doing? Yes, I would love a cup. Thanks. I hope you don't mind that I stayed here last night."

"Truth be told, I am so grateful that you did. I don't know how much help I would be to him right now with this chair thing. That was a mighty nice thing you did here."

Jimmy was still asleep while Lauren called his clients for that week and told them what happened. They were happy to reschedule when he was better and sent hopes that he would recover soon.

Cici was able to pick up more of the schedule and did a great job of filling in on the jobs she was comfortable with. Cici was happy to report that Mrs. Otterminder was happy that Jimmy was okay. The table could be fixed later.

A few hours later, Jimmy finally started waking up. He was hungry and starting to feel the pain in his arm return.

"Dad? Are you awake? Where are you? " Jimmy called from his recliner.

Papa Joe wheeled into the living room to check on his son.

"Glad to see you awake. That was quite a tumble you took yesterday. How are you feeling? Are you hungry?"

Jimmy smiled through the pain, "Does a goat stink? Hell, yes, I'm hungry!"

He laughed at his son, knowing that his sense of humor didn't go away—nor did his appetite. He was going to be just fine.

"Fantastic, son, I'll get you some coffee and Lauren will be around in a minute to get you taken care of."

"She's here?" Jimmy was surprised.

"Yeah, she stayed all night on the couch making sure you were okay. That's one fine woman there. Make sure you don't screw this one up."

"Dad! I didn't screw it up the last time either." Jimmy made a face at Papa Joe.

"We better get some coffee in you before you get cranky!" Papa Joe answered with a chortle, knowing that there was no way for his son to respond to that without sounding cranky.

"I am not cranky!" Jimmy exclaimed.

"See, cranky!" Papa Joe laughed as he wheeled back into the kitchen to get his son some much-needed coffee.

"Looks like someone has a case of the cranks!" Lauren needled him as she entered the living room.

"I'm not cranky! I'm in pain!"

She kissed him on the cheek and gave him two pills and a glass of water before he got his coffee. "This will help out with the pain."

After a few sips of coffee, Jimmy asked about his client.

"Did I do any major damage? Did Cici go and clean up and collect my tools? Are they okay?"

"Yes, Cici went by and checked in on things. The dining room table took the brunt of the ladder, but everything else seems to be okay. Mrs. Otterminder was more concerned about you than about her table. Cici replaced the lights and everything is cleaned up."

"What? Are you kidding me? Mrs. Otterminder is so nice. I feel really bad that this happened in her house. I am glad she didn't have to find me on the floor or hear it happen. How long will I be out of work? Oh, and Cici was great for filling in, too. Remind me to let her know how much I appreciate that."

Lauren took a sip of her coffee before answering. "Doctor said you will be out about six weeks before you can really start using that arm again. Plus, you will have to do physical therapy. You are lucky that it doesn't require any surgery. Before you complain about work, I have already called your clients and have postponed your bigger jobs. I booked Cici on all the appointments that she can do. It's a good thing it's still summer and she's around full-time!"

Jimmy was stunned and not sure what to say next. He was quiet for a little bit while he processed what she just said. Sitting still for him was going to be hard. He was used to fending for himself. Plus, there was still a month of summer left. He was grateful to Cici for being able to pick up the slack. Most of all, he could not believe that Lauren was doing all this stuff for him. He didn't know what to say just yet, but that warm feeling that had been in his tummy for a little while was starting to get much warmer now.

She continued, "You will be just fine. Keeping you from trying to do too much too soon will be the biggest challenge. You will have to give your shoulder time to heal, regardless of the ants in your pants."

Papa Joe interjected, "Son, you had better do as she says."

As Jimmy sat in his chair, he realized he was grateful for a few other things. His injured arm was not his dominant arm, so he could still do a lot more than if it were the other way around.

* * * * *

Later, Jimmy pulled out his trusty leather journal.

Dear Mom,

You are not going to believe this. Lauren stuck around and took care of me after the ladder crash. I am going to be grateful for her help in the next little while, too, because I will be at half speed for a bit. Nobody asked her; she just did it. Who does that? Well maybe

you would have. Oh, yeah, for sure you would
have. Don't jinx it now but...

* * * * *

Jimmy had heard about Gracie and called Calvin to
check and see how he was doing. He also wanted to let
Calvin know that Cici was doing a great job.

Calvin told him about Cassie and that they may be on
to something as a couple.

Of course, Calvin offered to help Jimmy out any way
he could while he was laid up.

* * * * *

Jimmy was nervous about showing up for his first
day of physical therapy. He wasn't a fan of pain and it
seems that those were the stories that he heard most from
people. He had Lauren drop him off because he still
couldn't drive yet. She wanted to come with him but he
insisted therapy was something he had to do on his own.
She knew he was right and didn't push the issue any
further.

He was the first one in the waiting room at 9:00 a.m.
The receptionist was cheery for a Monday morning. She
was old enough that she had certainly seen her share of
patients over the years and her silver hair showed it. She
wore it well and didn't seem like the type that would try
to cover it up. The name on her scrubs was "Penny."

"Hi, Jimmy. Thanks for showing up on time. Do you
have your insurance card?

Jimmy fumbled out his wallet with his good arm and
handed it over.

"Hi, Penny. It's nice to finally put a name with a face. Your hair looks great, by the way."

Her eyes opened a little wider to reveal a hint of blue. A smile came across her face as she blushed. In her position, she was more used to patients being rude and nasty to her. She understood that most were in pain, but that didn't excuse them from being rude.

"Oh, Jimmy, that is the nicest thing I have heard in a while. It's a wonder you are still single." She paused for a moment. "You are single, right?" she asked with a smile.

It was now Jimmy's turn for his cheeks to redden. "No, I'm not single anymore."

"Lucky girl! Now, go have a seat, and Dr. Sally will be right out for you."

A couple of hours later, Lauren came to pick up Jimmy. He walked out with his shirt wrinkled and sweaty, his hair mussed, and one shoe untied.

"Holy Moly, Jimmy, what did they do to you? You look worn out!"

"Did anyone ever tell you that physical therapists are the devil? She put the hurt on me for two hours, all the time with a smile. What the f—?"

Lauren started laughing. "Jimmy, I know all about PT because I have had some myself. You have to do it or you won't get that arm back."

Jimmy looked back at her with an all-knowing grimace on his face. "Yeah, I know I have to do it, and I can, and will. I just wanted to bitch a little about it. I won't bitch about it after this, but I had to get it off my chest. At least she is cute, so that will make it bearable." His frown turned into a grin as he teased her. Lauren just shook her head slightly and rolled her eyes.

"Hey, get this. You are going to love this one. She said I have to start doing yoga as part of my therapy," Jimmy said, grinning.

"Really? This, I gotta see. I'll sign up with you and we can do it together."

Jimmy gave her the weirdest look. "You want to be there, too? Uhm. Maybe not. This is still something I have to do on my own, and I'm gonna feel awkward enough in a room full of bendy women. I don't need you there, too. It's really sweet that you offered, but I am not ready for that yet."

Lauren's face fell. Although she was a little hurt by that, she saw his point. She just wanted the best for Jimmy. She had met his dad only recently and they hadn't yet discussed whether they were or were not yet an official couple. She saw it already, and she was sure that Jimmy saw some of it, but he was still being guarded about where his heart was.

Chapter 12: Namaste

There was a yoga studio not far from Jimmy's house. Their online reviews were pretty good, so Jimmy went by for a visit.

Upon opening the door, it was warm and inviting. Incense and music filled his senses. The lady at the desk was also one of the instructors. After listening to his purpose for being there, she recommended a beginner's class that he could start the next day.

The following morning, he found a spot in the back. After taking off his shoes and socks, he settled on his mat, like the rest of the students. The instructor came in and sat down cross-legged. Everyone else followed suit, including Jimmy.

"We are going to being this morning with an audible exhalation. Take in a deep breath and let it out with a sigh."

He took in a deep breath, and just as he was about to let it out, everyone around him forcefully blew out their breath with a loud "AHHHHHHHH." He furrowed his eyebrow as he looked around. Jimmy wondered silently to himself, *Who sighs like that?* He followed along with the rest of the class, doing his best to imitate those around him.

While he had no idea what a mudra was, he wasn't about to close his eyes either, because he wanted to make sure he was doing the poses correctly—at least, to the best of his ability. The good-looking woman next to him seemed to have them down pretty well. He thought to himself, *I don't think I will ever be that bendy.*

In the final resting stage, the lights were low and everyone was lying down, much like taking a nap in grade school, just without the cookies beforehand. He was going over what he had just done when someone near him farted. He did his best to not get the church giggles. With one eye open, he saw the instructor, Abby, walking around. He made sure not to look at her. If he did, he would completely lose it and burst out laughing. Thankfully, he made it through, and the lights came back up.

Abby walked over to him after class. He was struggling to put his socks and shoes back on.

"Hi, Jimmy. So, what did you think about your first class? It looked like you were doing all right for your first time."

"It was fun, actually, and I can see where a lot of people benefit from this. But I almost lost it at the end during the… uh, what do you call it?" Jimmy wrangled his left foot into his sock.

"Savasana."

"Yeah, someone close to me broke some wind and I almost got the church giggles." The instructor started laughing, which relieved Jimmy, so he started laughing, too.

"It's bound to happen when a bunch of people start moving their bodies around and parts inside get a little jumbled. I saw you over there with your shoulders shaking. I figured something was up. If she knew that you knew, she would have been mortified."

"Oh, no, you saw that? I am so glad you didn't come over or make eye contact. I was about to lose it."

"Everyone goes through that, and it's perfectly fine. Will you come again?"

"I think so. I can see where this will be good for my arm and my flexibility. I'm not ready to quit working just yet." Jimmy finished with his last shoe and Abby offered him her hand to help him up, which he accepted.

"Thanks."

"No problem. See you soon!"

* * * * *

Later that day, Calvin dropped by Jimmy's house to see how he was doing. You know you are best friends when your buddy walks in the door with a six-pack of your favorite beer.

Calvin cracked open the first beer and handed it to Jimmy.

"Hey, I wanted to talk to you about what it's like to own a business. I've got an idea for making custom sidecars like the one I made for Gracie, and I think it could go somewhere good."

Jimmy sat up in his chair, visibly excited. There was nothing like helping someone else explore their idea of being self-employed. Sure, it is hard work, but the rewards are much better than having "just a job."

They talked awhile about Gracie, sidecars, and even the latest on Cassie.

Jimmy was proud of his friend and excited about what his future held.

* * * * *

A few weeks later, on a beautiful autumn day in 2014, Papa Joe fetched the mail when it arrived. A letter from Jimmy's doctor was in the stack.

Papa Joe couldn't help himself any longer and was about to open the letter from the doctor when Jimmy walked through the back door.

"Dad? Were you just about to open my doctor's mail? I will let you read it when I'm done, if it's what I hope it is."

"Who me?" Papa Joe feigned innocence with the letter still in his hand and the letter opener on his lap in the wheelchair. Caught red-handed, he could only grin the famous Papa Joe grin that got him out of—and into—so much trouble when he was younger. "I was just getting it lined up for you!"

Jimmy snatched the letter and opened it. He had finished all of his physical therapy and was actually enjoying going to the yoga classes.

"Well, Jimmy, my boy, see what the doctor has to say!" Both men were hoping that the letter had good news in it.

Jimmy rolled his eyes at his dad and laughed. He knew better but wasn't gonna give him too hard of a time.

"C'mon, get to it, man!"

Jimmy opened the letter and quietly read it. With a frown on his face, he sat down. A look of dejection poured all over his face. He read it again and let out a heavy sigh. Still moving slowly, he got up and went to the bar, then took out two glasses and poured himself and his dad a drink.

"James Peter Harper, tell me what's in that letter right now." Papa Joe's parent voice became louder and demanding as his impatience rose. Every kid knows when the parents use the whole name, it's getting real.

Jimmy turned around and handed his dad a glass. With as somber a face as ever, he began to read the letter.

"This letter is to inform you that you are eligible to return to full work duty status."

"Goddammit, Jimmy, you had me going there, about to give me a heart attack." Papa Joe started laughing.

Jimmy also had a big smile on his face, knowing that he well and truly got his dad.

"That's for attempting to open my mail. Payback's a bitch!"

"Yeah, yeah, yeah. You had better let Lauren know. She has been worried about it, too."

"Yeah, I know, Dad. She was going to be my first call."

"Who was going to be your first call?" queried Lauren as she came through the back door. She had a handful of groceries for Papa Joe and put the bags on the countertop.

"Well, James Peter, you'd better tell her."

Lauren's eyes opened wide. She had never heard Jimmy's middle name spoken out loud. *And why are they drinking in the middle of the day?*

Jimmy turned around and winked at Papa Joe as he reached for another glass and began to slowly fill it with bourbon. Papa Joe played along and silently handed her the letter from the doctor with as somber a face as he could manage.

She frowned as she pulled her glasses down from her head and began to read.

"What? Oh, my God, that's great!" she exclaimed, without looking up. She paused to lower the letter and look at the guys in front of her. They could no longer keep their faces straight.

"You guys! What the hell is wrong with you? Are you trying to scare me? Just for that, I'm leaving the ice cream on the back porch to melt!" Lauren busied herself helping Papa Joe put the groceries away.

Papa Joe complained, "Don't punish me 'cause your boyfriend is a practical joker."

Jimmy piped up, looking at Lauren. "Well, since I got the all-clear from the doc, I want to go out and celebrate. Plus, I have some ideas that I want to talk to you about."

"Oh, Jimmy, that sounds great!" The pitch went up in her voice and then suddenly lowered. "It's not gonna be one of those 'we need to talk' talks is it?"

Jimmy heard the change in her voice and saw the worried look on her face. He was very quick to put her at ease.

"Lauren—" Jimmy only used her real name when he wanted to make a serious point. "This is not one of those talks at all and I hope I never have to say those words to you, ever. That's like getting called into the boss's office to get yelled at or the principal's office at school. Nothing good ever comes after that chat. Sweetie, this is all good stuff."

Lauren, feeling relieved, now had a smile on her face. "Where are we going to go? What do you feel like doing?"

"It's been a while since we did dinner 'right.' I was thinking about Captain's."

"Oh, wow, are you serious? That's one of my favorite places!"

"Yes. I'll make a reservation for us. I'll text you the time and pick you up later."

Lauren beamed.

* * * * *

Captain's was a classic old-school steakhouse with red leather booths and waiters wearing white shirts, bow ties, and full aprons. The place was known to be favorited by the local mafia back in the 1970s. Many of the most powerful and influential people in town still did a lot of business there.

As Jimmy was getting ready and trying to remember how to tie his happy-faced tie, he recalled a chat he had had with his father a few years ago.

"Jimmy, one fact of life—besides taxes and death—is that you will always be waiting on a woman. In the beginning, it is tough and annoying. However, it has also been my experience that the wait is worth it. They are just trying to look their best."

Finally ready, Jimmy headed to Lauren's.

He knocked on her door and lost his breath when she opened it.

The blue lapis silk dress showed off her body very nicely, while the spaghetti straps revealed a few tattoos that he had not yet seen.

Her long red hair, which was normally up in a messy bun, flowed all around her shoulders.

She saw his face drop and it put a big smile on hers.

"Well, hello, Mr. Handsome. It's nice to know I can still get your attention."

"Oh, wow, sweetie. You look amazing. My dad was right."

"Oh, about what, may I ask?"

"You will always be waiting on a woman and it will be worth it."

"Your dad is a wise old man. You better listen to him."

"We should go before we change our minds and want dessert first." Jimmy smiled and batted his eyelashes just for fun.

Lauren playfully punched him on the arm. "Oh, Jimmy! You are impossible!"

While at dinner, between steak, salad, and wine, Jimmy started to talk about things that had been on his mind.

"I've been so busy working the last five years trying to build up the business to where it is now. I like where it is at, and the phone keeps ringing. Being scheduled a few weeks out on a regular basis has been very comforting, income-wise. However, while I was laid up, I had time to think about a lot of stuff."

Lauren took a sip from her glass and looked over the rim at Jimmy.

"What's on your mind, Jimmy?"

"It seems to me that the whole reason we are in business for ourselves is so that we can have more time to enjoy life, right? Now that I have Cici working for me, I fully intend to start marking days on the calendar when I will not be working and instead doing something for me or my family. I have loads of ideas for fun things to do, and I would really like for those things to include you, too. I cannot tell you how much it meant to me for you to stay with me and my dad while I was really injured. That was priceless and will never be forgotten."

"Jimmy, I was happy to do it, and was glad that it was me taking care of you and your dad more than anyone else."

"I want to say something and it is probably going to come out goofier than it sounds in my head. Let me just get it out, before you say anything."

"Okay." She leaned forward with her chin on her clasped hands.

"I've not dated a whole lot, and a good majority of the times when I did, things went sideways. We haven't officially dated or really gone on any dates either, but we have worked together on a few projects and they went really well. Spending that working time with you was better than any date I could imagine. I think we have something special and I would like to see where it goes. Would it be okay if I called you my girlfriend?"

Lauren looked at Jimmy for a long moment, which felt like an eternity.

"There must be something in the air. I was talking to my BFF, Joni, about you at lunch the other day and she said almost the same thing. So, it's been on my mind, too.

"To tell you the truth. Jimmy, I can't think of anything better than for us to be officially a couple. Yes, I would be proud to be your girlfriend."

Jimmy looked at her with the biggest grin on his face.

"What would you say to going on a campout together? I am thinking about buying a camper so I can stay out in the woods a little longer than just being in a tent. I've done the tent thing for a while, and that's old now. Do you think you might wanna go camper shopping with me? I'm kinda hoping that you will also go on some of these adventures with me. Plus, it's not too late in the year to go camping. It's still the fall. And with the cooler weather coming, it's best to stay in a camper than in a tent."

"Jimmy Harper! How do you go from asking to be my boyfriend right to camping?"

She leaned back in her chair and laughed. "Only you, Jimmy."

"See? I told you I'm not good at that mushy romance stuff. I'm sorry. It should be a helluva first date though, right?" Jimmy had a big grin on his face.

Lauren took a drink of her wine and shook her head at him while she smiled back.

"Jimmy, Jimmy, Jimmy. You are impossible! Uh, did you forget about the camper in my backyard? It's in great shape. There's no reason to go buy another one."

"Oh, yeah. I totally forgot about that. That would be great. Wow, you're on board with this. I thought it was going to be a much harder sell than this." He sat back and laughed.

"Well, Jimmy, my boy, we aren't getting any younger. We may as well do it while we have the means and ways to make it happen."

"Okay. Let's go to Payson. It's close enough for a shakedown trip just to make sure that everything works, especially since it's been sitting for a little bit. If you have the manuals, I will start looking it over tomorrow to make sure it's travel worthy."

* * * * *

Dear Mom,

I can call her my girlfriend now. Yeah, I know, ME, right?! I wasn't as smooth as maybe Dad would have been, but it was me. We didn't do a lot of dating but I don't think we needed to. Just her working with me on the Cat Project and her helping us out after my big fall says way more than a few dates ever could, I think. Dad says that you would like her, too. Actually, I'm sure you'd love her.

* * * * *

Just as Calvin had promised, he had lunch at The Coffee Stand with the first couple from the bike show.

They came to an agreement and Calvin accepted his first deposit on making a sidecar for someone else.

After he deposited the check through his bank's mobile app, he framed and hung it on the wall in his shop right under a picture of Gracie.

A week after that, Cassie helped him build a website and do all of the other official things needed to properly start a business.

They were shoulder to shoulder in front of his computer when Cassie said, "Well, Calvin, honey, your website is ready to go. All you need to do is push the button and you'll be live." She smiled and pushed the mouse toward him.

"Are you sure this will work?" He was hesitant.

"Yes, I am sure of it, and so are you, or else you would not have taken that deposit."

"Yeah, I suppose you are right. I'm just doing a gut check. Okay, here goes." He put his hand slowly over the mouse and one click later, his website came to life.

Cassie went into the kitchen and came out with a bottle of champagne and two glasses.

"Calvin, I am so proud of you! This is an amazing thing and calls for a celebration."

POP! The cork went flying across the room.

"I've always wanted to do that," she said, then laughed as she poured each of them a glass.

Chapter 13: Happy Campers

By the end of the week, Jimmy had gone through Lauren's camper and checked the tires, water lines, and power supply. Everything seemed in working order.

It was Saturday at first light when Jimmy backed his truck up to the trailer and got connected. He made sure that the trailer wasn't more than what his truck could reasonably haul. He even practiced driving around with it, to be sure. He hated seeing those trailers on the side of the road that were obviously too large for the truck that was towing them.

With coffee in hand and caffeinated smiles on their faces, they hit the road.

Everything was going along just fine, until… BAM!

There was a loud pop outside the truck window and the truck got wobbly. With the wheel shaking in his hand, Jimmy pulled the truck and trailer to a stop on the side of the road, thankful for the large shoulder. It made it safer to pull off there.

Lauren was still gripping the "Oh-shit" bar with white knuckles as he got out to look things over.

The back tire on his truck was completely shredded.

"Dammit! We didn't even make it thirty minutes out of town. I must have hit something on the road. I checked them all before we headed out. Good thing I checked the spare. Guess I will get to it."

It would be a little more annoying to change with the trailer attached to his truck, but it wasn't his first flat tire. He put on his gloves, got to work, and within half an hour, the spare was on and they were back on the highway.

There was a rest area about five miles up the road, so he pulled in.

"Oh, crap, what's wrong now?" Lauren exclaimed, obviously frustrated. It seemed as though some of the wind was taken out of her sails.

"Nothing is wrong. I just wanted to pull over to make sure the lug nuts are still tight. It's what you are supposed to do after changing a flat."

"Oh, okay, that makes sense. Good thing we are stopping. I gotta pee."

They only stayed long enough for both of them to take care of that.

"Okay, mount up. Our little bit of trip drama is already over, so the rest of the trip should be awesome," Jimmy said with a smile and confidence in his voice. "Okay, let's see what's on the radio around here."

He fiddled with the tuner a bit until a station came in clearly.

Singing along with the radio, he belted out, "Summertimmmmmme and the liver is queasy!"

Lauren snapped her head around with her eyes wide open and started laughing.

"That is not the line, Jimmy."

"Sure it is. That's what it sounds like to me." With a grin, he continued, "Fisssh are jumpin', and the cousins are high."

Lauren laughed so hard that her shoulders were shaking, yet no noise came from her mouth. "Are you always this bad at singing?"

For a brief second, he took his hands off the wheel and made a fake angel hoop over his head.

"I don't know what you are talking about, sweetie," he grinned.

Lauren just shook her head at him while giving him a half-smile.

They spent the rest of the drive talking, listening to music, and having fun.

Their campsite was ready for them when they pulled in. He had tried to get a pull-through site, but they were already taken.

He wasn't the best at backing up with a trailer, although he spent some time that week practicing in a parking lot.

They pulled out the walkie-talkies they got to make communication better.

Lauren got out and helped instruct him which way to go while Jimmy maneuvered the trailer with his truck.

He got so off course with his second attempt that he almost backed the trailer into a picnic table.

"STOP!" Lauren yelled. No radio was needed for that one.

He jammed on the brakes and got out. Jimmy looked at the trailer, then the table's bench seat, and then Lauren.

"What?" She put her hands on her hips, daring him to challenge her.

"Nothing. Good call, Chief," he said, and held up his hand for a high-five.

She finally smiled. "I totally thought you were going to yell at me."

"Nope, I was driving, so that one would have totally been on me."

After a few more tries, they finally got it straight and Jimmy shut off the truck.

"I don't know how those semi-truck drivers do that all day long. I have a new respect for that skill. I will get it, too. I just need to keep practicing."

"Let's take a walk around the place to calm down after all that excitement," suggested Lauren. Jimmy grabbed her hand and off they went.

After they returned from their walk around the campground and had located the camp showers and country store, they got busy with setting up camp.

The wobble from the flat tire caused some of the things inside to fly around inside the trailer. The cupboard doors had opened and a box of cereal, some paper plates, and plastic cups were everywhere.

When Jimmy and Lauren opened the door and saw the mess, they sat down on the picnic bench in silence. They finally looked at each other with a grimace, then burst out laughing until their faces hurt. Some experienced nearby campers guessed what had happened, and the old couple in the next camping spot over was smiling and tapping their noses.

Lauren and Jimmy tidied everything up and made something to eat. They were fairly tired from the day's events, so they went straight to bed after that.

The next day was great. The weather was clear and cool, with not a cloud in the sky.

They made friends with some of the other campers and enjoyed being in the wilderness of the country and mountains.

That night, after the gas campfire was turned off and cooled down a little, they went to bed.

A few hours later, a thunderstorm had moved in with no warning. That often happened in the autumn up on the Mogollon Rim.

CRACK-K-K! FLASH!

The thunderclap shook the camper and Lauren bolted right up in bed. A downpour immediately followed. The young couple sleepily tried to get all the windows shut before it got wet inside. They were just a bit too late.

"Well, holy shit, Jimmy, what else is going to go wrong on this trip?"

Jimmy could see the exasperation on Lauren's face as she sat down with a towel in her hand.

"I don't know but I think we have had our quota. We should be fine tomorrow. Every new camping couple has to go through this. Think of it as an initiation." Jimmy tried to make light of the situation.

The thunder had passed. Now, there was just light rain peppering the roof of the camper. It was almost melodic as they snuggled under the comforter, lying in the soft glow from the fairy lights that lit the cabin.

Lauren was certainly not sleepy anymore.

"So, did you date much before me?"

Jimmy gave a slight chuckle. "Yeah, if you can call it dating. There were a few first dates, a very short relationship that ended as quickly as it began, and one clusterfuck."

Lauren raised her eyebrows at that. "Wow, I gotta hear about that one. Sounds like a good story."

Jimmy told her the story of the two girls who scammed a lunch out of him that one Friday.

Lauren sat there with her jaw down and eyes open. She was surprised and disgusted at the same time.

"Oh, shit, Jimmy, That's horrible. They were probably told by someone—or maybe even by social media—that the only men to look for are those making six figures and are some sort of doctor, lawyer, or something. Ashley didn't have a clue what was in front of her. That's too bad for her but very good for me!" She looked over at Jimmy and snuggled even closer.

"So, what about you? I'm sure you have some good college stories."

Lauren softly guffawed. "Well, there are two that come to mind. One is Robert. He was in my advanced accounting class. We had coffee a few times. He was smart, and dry funny for an accountant. He was going into the family real estate business right after graduation. On paper, we looked good, but there was no spark. That's as far as that got."

Jimmy looked over and nodded.

"Who was the other one?"

"Well, on the other side of the spectrum was the crazy and wild one. His name was Cruz and he was there on family money. He really just wanted to make his parents happy. He was the token bad boy, if you will. He had no solid plans after graduation except that he wanted to through-hike the Pacific Crest Trail before getting serious about life. I think he was crazy and strong enough to do it. It's a pretty big undertaking to walk twenty-six hundred miles across the country. Someday, I'd love to hear the tales about his adventures."

The two continued cuddling. Jimmy stroked her hair.

"I'm glad you are so honest with me about everything," Lauren whispered in his ear. "I love you, Jimmy."

He whispered back, "I love you, too."

* * * * *

Jimmy stayed awake a little while longer as Lauren faded off to sleep. He turned on the tiny reading light on his side and reached for his trusty journal.

Hi, Mom,

We are on our first campout. It's been crazy, with a flat tire and a surprise rainstorm. Who knows what's next?

I can't believe she said she loves me. She even said it first. I said it back, too. Now, if I can just keep it up and not do something stupid.

Jimmy put away his journal, snuggled up to Lauren, and finally fell asleep under the big blanket.

They slept until morning, when the roar of a diesel engine rudely woke them up. Jimmy hated diesels because they were noisy and smelly. Some owners loved to let them just idle, and the older ones rolled coal on the highway.

Still in pajamas, Jimmy got up and started the coffee. He stepped outside to survey the damage from the storm last night. One of the cracks they heard was a large tree branch that broke off and landed just inches from the back of their trailer.

"Holy shit, Lauren, come look at this."

With a coffee mug in hand and slippers on, she came out to see what Jimmy was talking about.

"Oh, crap, Jimmy. That thing is huge. I tell ya, we must be doing something right, or your guardian angel is still looking out for you. That could have done some serious damage." She rolled her eyes skyward and mouthed a "thank you" to his angel.

Jimmy couldn't stop being a handyman; it was just in his blood. After coffee, he got dressed and pulled out the small, cordless electric chainsaw he had packed along with a few other tools.

One of the other nearby campers came over to help out, and they had the tree chopped and cleared out in no time. Park Ranger Lisa came by with a box of donuts to thank them for helping out.

After all that, they decided to pack up since their venture was just a shakedown trip anyway. It was Monday morning and they wanted to get home. They had had enough shakes for one weekend.

They hit the road and made it into town without any further incidents. Jimmy pulled onto the street in front of Lauren's house.

Excited to be home, Lauren yelled, "Yay, we made it!"

He was getting ready to back into her driveway when they heard a POP and felt the truck vibrate. They both hopped out to see what the noise was all about.

One of the trailer tires had completely blown into tiny bits of rubber. *Not again!* Torn between being pissed off and laughing hysterically, Jimmy sat down on the curb to gather himself for a minute. He shook his head and wondered what happened.

Lauren took a closer look. "Goddammit!" Jimmy could hear the frustration in her voice. "Son of a bitch!" She waved a fist in the air.

He never figured she could cuss like that.

Staring at her, he didn't know whether he should burst out laughing or not. He was trying to keep it in. Just when he allowed himself to think she was cute when she got mad, he lost it and couldn't hold his laughter in any longer.

A smile came across Lauren's face. "Well, shit, Jimmy. I can't stay mad at the tire. At least it was kind enough to wait until we got home safely."

With only three tires left on the trailer, Jimmy slowly backed the trailer into the driveway.

"Shut it down. We are going inside and taking a nap. This can wait until later," Lauren declared.

Jimmy sighed a big sigh and held the door open for Lauren. He knew he wouldn't nap. He had work to do.

Chapter 14: The Other Redhead

The week was busy. Jimmy had adjusted his schedule to accommodate their getaway, but now that he was back, it was full, even with Cici helping out on the smaller jobs. Jimmy fixed a major plumbing leak, repaired a huge fence, and finished up some details on another cat castle construction.

Lauren's work week started off just fine. She was about to begin a new project for a big client in town. She was also redecorating a home after another client had a messy divorce. The poor lady didn't seem to have any other female friends to talk to, so Lauren got an earful of all the lady's trials and tribulations. Lauren managed to get her out of the house for a few days so she could work in peace. She had heard enough about bad men in her client's life.

It was finally Friday and her project with Ms. Grumpy was over with. Lauren went home early.

Stressed out and tired from the week, she drew a hot bath and poured a glass of wine to relax. She recalled what the lady had said and was very grateful that her Jimmy was not like the men that her client had described.

Later that day, she had a great idea: to cook a nice dinner for Jimmy, to show him how much she appreciated him, and that she did not want to take him for granted.

"Hey, Jimmy, what are you doing tomorrow night?"

"Hey, I have no idea. I think I'm just gonna hang out with my dad since I haven't seen him much this week. It's been a crazy one for me. For you, too, if I remember right."

"Well, I was thinking that I would like to make dinner for us, and then you can take home the leftovers to Papa Joe. How does that sound?"

"I have never been one to turn down a home-cooked meal. So, yes. I am in. What are you making and what can I bring?"

"It's a surprise, and you can bring dessert. Come over around six."

"Great. See you tomorrow!"

"Perfect!"

* * * * *

The next afternoon, Jimmy went to the grocery store to pick up supplies for a strawberry shortcake. He still had no idea what Lauren was making for dinner; she just said it would be one of his favorite dishes. Apparently, she had called Papa Joe earlier to find out what he liked.

Jimmy heard a voice behind him that he recognized, but it wasn't Lauren.

He turned around to see an old high school friend, Sonia.

"Jimmy! Is that you? Oh, my God, it is so good to see you! What's going on?" Sonia had been on the cheerleading squad in high school and still had the long wavy red hair that she did back then. She ran up and threw her arms around him, and then gave him a big kiss on the cheek.

"Sonia? Wow, what are you doing in town? It's great to see you, too." He wrapped his arms around her as he returned her great big hug.

"Jimmy, you still look so young. What's your secret?" Sonia asked flirtatiously.

"Oh, thanks. I let a neighborhood dog lick my face once a week." He winked back at her. They laughed and continued taking up space in the aisle with their arms still around each other as they chattered away. Other shoppers steered their carts around them as they shopped near the happy couple.

Lauren just happened to be at the same store and was at the far end of the aisle, just about to turn the corner into Jimmy's aisle when she heard the other redhead call out Jimmy's name. She ducked behind a large soda display so she would not be seen.

Her mind automatically began racing. Who was this other woman? With red hair, nonetheless! He never mentioned that he dated another redhead.

He said they were all blondes. She was so mad at the thought of her Jimmy seeing another woman behind her back that she left her cart right where it was.

Quickly and quietly, she left the store.

A few minutes later, Jimmy and Sonia said their goodbyes.

Jimmy finished his shopping and headed for home to make the dessert.

Later, Jimmy knocked on Lauren's door. He was five minutes late, which was out of character for him, but there had been a huge traffic jam on the way into her street.

Lauren met him at the door, wearing sweats. Her face was red and tear-stained.

She held the door open with one hand and had a glass of wine in her other hand.

"What are you doing here?" Lauren asked in the nastiest tone.

Jimmy was taken aback. This was a side of her that he'd never seen before.

"Shouldn't you be out with your other redheaded girlfriend? The one that you didn't tell me about?"

He was caught completely off guard.

This was certainly not the welcome he was expecting.

"What on earth are you talking about? I don't have any other girlfriend and certainly not a redheaded one!"

Jimmy looked confused as he wrinkled up his forehead, wondering what had come over her.

He quickly recalled running into Sonia at the store.

"Where did you see this supposed 'other girlfriend' of mine?"

"You were at the store today and practically smooching in the aisle. Everyone had to go around you. I was just about to come up that aisle when I saw you two with your arms around each other."

She still had a sneer on her face.

Jimmy recalled the hug with Sonia. He tried to get in a word edgewise to explain, but Lauren wasn't hearing any of it.

"Dinner is off tonight, so you can just go home. Maybe call up that other girl so your night is not a complete waste of time. Now, go away!"

"Will you at least let me explain?" Jimmy tried pleading with her.

"I do not want to hear it!" Her face was as red as her hair now.

Bewildered, he said, "You're serious, aren't you? Very well, then, my lady, I will let you be." Jimmy backed up a few steps and left the bag containing the dessert on the lawn. With both hands crossed and covering his heart, he looked her in the eyes, slowly bowed, and went back to his truck without another word.

Jimmy drove back home, still processing the weird encounter that just happened. He had never seen this side of her and was worried that she may have other traits that he should know about. He knew that he was in love with her, but was now second-guessing himself.

Papa Joe was surprised when Jimmy came home early. Just by the look on his face, he knew that something horrible had happened. He grabbed a few glasses along with the bourbon and met him on the porch. Jimmy filled him in on what happened at the store and Lauren's house.

* * * * *

On the other side of town, Lauren was on the phone with her best friend, Joni. Joni had met Jimmy a few times and liked him.

Lauren knew that she could always count on Joni to be the voice of reason, even if it wasn't what she wanted to hear.

"Joni, he just stood there not disagreeing with what I saw."

"So-o-o, did you give him a chance to explain his side before you slammed the door in his face?

"Uhm-m-m, well-l-l, no-o-o. But I saw what I saw, and I was so mad."

Joni let there be silence on the phone for a moment to emphasize her point.

"Don't you think you should have listened to the man? Has he ever given you a reason to doubt him? He's crazy about you! Even his dad loves you. Why would you screw that up? Did he really leave you with a bow? Wow, I'm impressed. Who does that anymore? Lauren, darling, you need to fix this, or he's gonna be gone forever."

* * * * *

Back on Jimmy's side of town, Papa Joe said, "Well, son, that was certainly unexpected and the craziest thing I have ever heard about a date going wrong. That's even crazier than the girl who tried to bring her friend along for free. What are you going to do? I would not have guessed she would act like that. It's very out of character."

"Dad, I have no idea. I am still floored at her reaction. I didn't do anything wrong at all. How do I know she hasn't been hiding this jealous streak in her all this time that we have been working together? What would happen if we got married and then the crazy lady came out? I just don't have time for that kind of drama in a life partner or wife."

"You need to talk to her, son."

"Maybe so, but she needs to make the next move. I think I am going to pack up some gear and head out for my favorite fishing hole for a few days. Cici has the schedule under control."

"The same one where we caught that monster striper? That was a fun day. That thing fed all three of us that day. Damn good eating, it was."

Papa Joe recalled the great day with his wife and son.

"Yep, same place. I'll be back on Monday sometime."

Papa Joe grinned.

"Maybe by that time, she will have had a bitchectomy!"

Jimmy burst out laughing.

"Dad! Should I order her some bitchicillin?"

It was the best laugh they have had in a while.

* * * * *

Dear Mom,

Holy shit. This thing may be over. I knew it was too good to be true. I saw the ugly side of her today and it was bad. I know I didn't do anything wrong this time. But I know why she thought I did. She saw me hugging an old friend in the store. She just jumped right over to the wrong conclusion without all of the facts. It really didn't seem like her.

But do you ever really truly know someone?

Maybe this jealous streak is what she has been hiding. If that's the case, I am outta here. I guess it's all up to her now.

* * * * *

The next morning, Lauren knocked on their door. She had changed into jeans and a T-shirt and tucked her hair under a baseball cap. She could hear Papa Joe roll to the door.

"Good morning, young lady."

"Hi, Papa Joe. I normally would have let myself in, but under the circumstances, that might have been a little disrespectful."

"I get that, for sure. Come on in. I just made a fresh pot of coffee."

"Thanks, Papa Joe, but this might need something a little stronger."

"Jimmy's not here right now."

"Yessir, I kinda figured that when I didn't see his truck. But it's okay. I can talk to you and get your advice on this."

Papa Joe put a splash of bourbon in their coffee cups and remained silent while she told the story of what happened. He listened, occasionally nodding his head.

"I'm mad at myself, more than anything, now. I think I blew it. What should I do? I don't want to lose Jimmy over this."

"Lauren, you are a grown woman, and I think you already know in your heart what you need to do. If you love my son like I think you do, then you need to go find him and make this right. I know he loves you. But that barrage of crap you laid on him last night damn near broke his heart."

Changing his demeanor from a grimace to curiosity, he asked, "Did he really give you a bow?" He let out a low whistle. "Yeah, you must have rightly pissed him off. He doesn't do that very often."

"Do you know where I can find him?"

"He asked me not to say where. The only thing I will say is that it's one of his favorite fishing holes."

"Thanks, Papa Joe. I'd better hurry up and go find him."

She gave him a kiss on the cheek and headed out the door. Once back in her car, she pulled up the GPS and tried to figure out which lake he would head for. There were a few nearby, so it was not going to be an easy search for her.

She made a beeline for her top guess and soon pulled onto the dirt road leading down to the lake. There were not many camping spots, so it didn't take long to figure out that he was not there.

She headed back down the highway to her second guess, another 30 miles down the road. It was a state-run park, so after paying for a day pass, she asked the female ranger if she might have seen his truck. She wasn't sure because she had only just come on duty.

The lake was much busier with campers, so Lauren just started a clockwise drive through the park and hoped she got lucky.

She finally spotted his truck parked in an empty spot near his camp. She still wasn't sure what she was going to say to him and was relieved when he wasn't around. His fishing pole and tackle box were missing and there was still a pot of coffee on the firepit grill.

She sat down in a chair near the firepit to wait for him. She realized why he liked this spot. Despite the busy campground, it was still quiet and peaceful. There were a few puffy white clouds in the sky, and the quacking of some faraway ducks on the lake was the only sound she heard. The tranquility calmed her and she soon dozed off.

Jimmy spotted her truck on his walk in from the lake. He wasn't sure how she found him, but he had a pretty good guess as to what she was doing here, so he snuck into the camping spot from another direction. Once he got closer, he realized he didn't have to sneak in because she was fast asleep.

Although he had not sorted out his feelings about her and what all went on the other day, he couldn't resist the chance to have some fun at her expense.

He quietly reached into the cooler and pulled out a beer. From behind her chair, he popped the top on it with a big "whoosh" right next to her ear. She screamed in an effort to get away from whatever was behind her. She rolled out of the chair and onto the ground.

Jimmy could not stop laughing as she scowled at him. The harder she scowled, the harder he laughed until he had to sit down in the other chair and catch his breath. Knowing that she had been royally had, a slow smile crept in to replace the scowl.

"What are you doing here?" He offered her the open beer. "Did my dad tell you where I was?"

"No. I went by your house this morning to talk to you. All he said was that you went fishing and wouldn't be back until Monday. I feel so bad about what I said and didn't want to wait until then to resolve things."

Lauren took the beer from his hand, righted her chair, sat down across from him, and looked deep into his eyes.

"Jimmy, I am really sorry for the awful things I said to you and for refusing to listen to your side of the story. If you never want to talk to me again, I will understand and leave, without any drama. Papa Joe told me the other side of the story, and I am an idiot."

Jimmy sat quietly, listening.

After a few moments of silence, he said, "I am still not sure what to think about that. You said some really mean things and you didn't even take the time to hear my side of it. I almost gave you back your house key right there. The worst part was that you immediately assumed the worst before you heard all the facts."

Lauren sighed and said, "I know. I'm really sorry." She bowed her face in shame. Jimmy took a long pull off his beer before he continued talking.

"You damn near broke my heart. You should know me well enough by now to know that I don't mess around. The fact that you are here is a plus for you. If I had gone home tomorrow without any word from you, I am not sure if we would ever talk again."

She looked up at him with tears in her eyes. Quietly she asked, "Does that mean that you still wanna see me?"

She was almost afraid to hear his answer.

There were tears in his eyes, too, as he looked her straight in the eye and gently nodded his head.

Lauren stood up. "I am truly sorry. You will never see that side of me ever again."

Jimmy stood up with his arms outstretched.

"Come here."

She leapt up and into his arms. They hugged so tightly that her feet came off the ground. As soon has her feet touched down again, he took her face in his hands and slowly kissed her.

Unbeknownst to them, a small crowd had been forming on the outside of their campsite. During their discussion, Jimmy and Lauren didn't even notice.

One old lady piped up, "It's about time you kissed her! What took you so long?"

Another one echoed her with, "That's a good man there. Don't blow it again, darling."

Their faces flushed red as they turned around to see the crowd in front of them.

"Oh, damn, I guess we were louder than we figured!" Jimmy laughed. "What do you say we break camp and head for home?"

"Sounds good. Jimmy, I love you so much."

"Lauren Perry, I love you, too."

Chapter 15: The Crazy Neighbor

Months passed.

During the Christmas holidays, Lauren's father, Finn, met the Harpers. All of them got along well. Finn was happy that his little girl finally met someone who captured her heart. Papa Joe and the Irishman shared quite a few stories and laughs. Everyone had a great time.

Now, it was nearly spring of 2015. The February weather was warm enough in Phoenix that their friends in Canada were jealous. While Canadians in Ontario suffered freezing cold temperatures, Americans in the south-western part of the United States enjoyed walking around with only a light jacket on—if they wore a jacket at all!

One day, Jimmy went to check the mailbox. They didn't get much mail because Jimmy paid most of his bills online. So, he only checked it every other day or so. Besides the normal junk mail, political flyers, and credit card offers, there was a letter from their landlord's holding company. It reminded them that their lease would be up in a month but the rent was going to increase by $300 per month. Both Jimmy and Papa Joe were shocked and maddened.

They had been good tenants for years, paid their rent on time, and caused no problems. Maybe a small escalation would be reasonable, but such a huge increase was certainly closer to highway robbery.

The next morning, Jimmy went to work and Papa Joe wheeled himself down to the property manager's office to have a word with them. He liked the previous manager but a few months ago, she had disappeared. Now, there was a much younger lady in charge, and she seemed to have an attitude.

For some reason, she rubbed Papa Joe the wrong way. He wasn't sure what the reason was. Maybe he was too old, or maybe because she wasn't comfortable around someone in a wheelchair. Whatever it was, Papa Joe felt it.

"Hi, Mr. Harper. What can I help you with today?"

"You sent me this note that says my lease will be up in a month and that you are raising the rent by three hundred dollars. Why? We haven't caused you any grief, we pay our rent on time—or even early." By the frown on Papa Joe's face, she could tell he was serious.

"Yes, sir. Everyone is getting these notices, not just you. There are new owners that bought the company a few months ago as an investment. The manager before me disagreed with such a high increase, so they fired her."

"Well, that's a bunch of shit!"

Looking like she had given this speech before, she continued, although it wasn't comfortable for her. "I wish I had a say in the matter, but I don't. I am really sorry. Many other residents are just finding out now, too."

"Well, young lady, while it may be legal for your bosses to do this, it sure ain't ethical or moral. It's downright sleazy and greedy. It's too bad they have to hide behind you to do this. I am going to talk to my son and decide tonight if we are going to stay or not. It's a shame that you couldn't find someone nicer to work for. You seem pretty sharp for a young'un. Good day!"

Papa Joe spun around in his wheelchair and headed for the door.

Jimmy went home around lunchtime that day.

He wanted to check on his dad.

He listened while Papa Joe told him about that morning's drama.

Jimmy looked at his dad and smiled.

"Hey, what's with the smiley face, son? This is serious."

"Yeah, Dad, I know. It's just nice to see that you still have some fire left in you. Poor girl didn't know who she was messing with. We will figure something out. We usually do. I can start looking for rentals in the morning and asking around to people I know. By the way, Lauren wants us to come over for dinner tonight. I think she wants to make up to us both for this past weekend. Be ready around five."

"Jimmy, I wish more young people were like you and Lauren. Too many of them are so selfish, self-absorbed, and have no work ethic. On a more pleasant note, I can't wait to see Lauren's house. From your stories, it sounds like a cool one. I will be ready."

* * * * *

Later that day, Jimmy and Papa arrived at Lauren's house.

Papa Joe saw the circular driveway and was immediately impressed. Lauren gave him the dime tour of the main floor and showed him the guest house in the backyard. It was connected to the house with a wide breezeway that was easily navigable by wheelchair.

She caught Papa Joe with a curious look on his face as he rolled around the place.

"So, how did you come about this house?" Papa Joe asked.

"Well, it belonged to my mother before she got married to my dad. He just never had the heart to sell it. I think he was hoping to give it to me someday, and he did, when I came back to town."

Lauren rolled him into the kitchen from the breezeway. Upon opening the door, the smell of chicken-fried steak hit him in the nose.

"Uh-oh, Jimmy, we had better watch out. She must've done something horrible if she is making us chicken-fried steak." He winked at Jimmy just as Lauren fake complained.

"Hey, Papa Joe!"

They all burst out laughing. The guys took their places at the dining room table as Lauren readied their plates. She brought out a bottle of wine, too.

Before they started to eat, Lauren spoke up.

"Papa Joe and Jimmy, I wanted to have you over for dinner tonight to say how sorry I am for last weekend. I still feel badly and embarrassed by my actions. I hope you can forgive me. I really love both of you and it would be sad if you were gone from my life."

Papa Joe smiled and raised his glass.

"My dear Lauren, it has been wonderful having you in both of our lives. It has saved us both from being dull and boring. The matter is forgotten and won't be discussed again."

All three raised and clinked their glasses.

It wasn't long before the topic of rent came up.

Lauren listened while Papa Joe retold his story of that morning's drama. Suddenly, she had a goofy look on her face, like she had the idea of the century.

"Jimmy, can you see me in the kitchen for a moment? Papa Joe, excuse us for a minute, would you, please?"

Jimmy and Papa Joe exchanged glances and shrugged shoulders like they both had no idea of what was to come next. Papa Joe motioned for them to go as Jimmy tentatively said, "Sure."

Once Lauren got Jimmy in the pantry, she wrapped her arms around him and kissed him.

"That was because I love you, and this one is because I have a brilliant plan." She kissed him again. Jimmy was beginning to like this idea, whatever it was.

Papa Joe yelled from the dining room, "Hey, if you went back there just to make out with my son, you could have at least given me the remote!"

Jimmy and Lauren turned red and laughed.

"Okay, you've got my attention. What's on your mind?" Jimmy asked.

She lowered her voice and laid out her plan to her boyfriend. She was sure her father would approve.

Jimmy scratched his head for a moment as he mulled it over.

"Holy shit, that is brilliant! I just wonder if he will go for it. I like it, though."

* * * * *

"Okay, clear the plates and I will get started with dessert."

Lauren came back in a few minutes later with the strawberry shortcake, a bottle of champagne, and three champagne flutes.

Papa Joe was looking at Lauren with a discerning eye as she popped the cork on the champagne and poured bubbly liquid into the three glasses.

"Papa Joe, I have a solution to your rent problem and I believe that Jimmy is on board, too." She handed him a glass. "Now, before you say anything, hear me out." Papa Joe waited eagerly with curiosity.

"It's been a helluva week and I want to let you know that I really do love you for letting me into your lives. I have this giant house here and nothing would make me happier than for the two of you to move in. Papa Joe, you can have the guest house to yourself. We will remodel and make any changes you need or want for the wheelchair access and such. My house is paid for, so there will be no rent. You can take that rent money and do something fun with it."

Stunned, Papa Joe looked at Jimmy for a minute.

"Did you put her up to this?"

"No! I just found out about this, right when you accused us of playing kissy-face in the kitchen."

They all burst out laughing.

"You must have read my mind because as you were giving me the tour, I was thinking that this would be a cool house to live in. So, yes, I think it would be a dandy idea. When do we move in?" A big smile crossed his face.

"Lauren and I will get started on the remodeling for the guest house. I figure it will take about a week or so to get it all done. Then you can have all the fun in telling that little manager girl that you are moving out and the new owners can stuff it."

Papa Joe was on a roll with ideas now. "Do you think I could even get one of those electric chairs? Maybe we can put flames on the side? How about a roll-in shower?"

Lauren started laughing. "Woah, wait a minute, Papa Joe. We gotta get the thing built first, then you can go 'Mario Andretti' anywhere you want."

* * * * *

Dear Mom,

Wow. If you could see us now. We are all moving in together in Lauren's big house. It was even her idea. She is never short of surprises. I am still floored. I think I am going to have to ask her to marry me soon. I am sure you would have already asked me why I have not asked her yet.

* * * * *

A week later, all of the renovations had been done and it was finally moving day.

Lauren's neighbor, Marilyn, hadn't paid Lauren much attention to her in the few years she was there alone. However, once Jimmy and Papa Joe moved in, she became increasingly nosy.

On one of the moving days, she just appeared out of nowhere and walked into their garage.

Giving herself the self-guided tour, she began eyeballing Jimmy's tools and equipment.

Jimmy walked into the garage with two boxes in his arms. He stopped immediately when he saw the stranger with gray hair there.

"I hope you aren't planning to use all this noisy equipment all hours of the day. There's a noise ordinance you know," quipped Marilyn.

"Umm, who are you, and what are you doing in my garage?" Jimmy asked sternly after putting his boxes down.

"Oh, I'm Marilyn, your neighbor. I was just curious as to what all the commotion over here was all about."

Standing up to his full height and just within a few feet of her, he continued, "You still haven't answered my questions as to who you are and what you are doing in my garage, uninvited."

She tried continued to dodge him by asking more of her own questions, as if she never heard him at all.

"Do you kids even have jobs?"

With his hands on his hips in front of Marilyn's five-foot frame, he continued to move toward her, making her a little fidgety.

"Ma'am, this is not the best way to introduce yourself. I don't want you underfoot. We will be moving a lot of stuff in, and you might get run over. Please go home and maybe we will come around soon for a proper howdy-do."

Marilyn scoffed and raised her eyebrows at him.

"You can't tell me what to do. Who do you think you are talking to?"

Jimmy inched even closer to her as he pointed to the garage door.

"Well, Ma'am, you are in my house and my property as an uninvited guest, and thus, you are trespassing. So, yes, I can tell you to leave. I won't ask nicely again. You need to leave right now."

She finally got the hint and backed her way out of the garage, nearly tripping over a box of books.

"Well," she harrumphed, "I never..." Her sentence trailed off as she scurried down the driveway to her own house.

Lauren appeared holding a cold can of pop and asked, "What was that all about?"

"The nosy Karen—or Marilyn, as she calls herself—from down the street, was roaming around through our garage. She even had the nerve to ask if we had jobs. She got upset when I told her she was trespassing and needed to leave immediately. What the heck?"

Lauren laughed.

"You know, I had heard a couple of rumors about her but had never met her. I guess the rumors were true. Well, things just got more interesting."

Jimmy was still a little hot under the collar as he took the cold soda that Lauren offered him.

An evil grin suddenly crossed her face. Rubbing her chin and squinting her eyes, she said in a low voice, "Ooh, I think we are going to have a little bit of fun with her."

Jimmy caught on quickly. In an equally menacing voice, he answered, "Ooh, yes! What did you have in mind for this little Karen?"

"I am not sure, but it will have to be epic. Let me talk to the other neighbors and see what kind of dirt I can dig up on her. People are so much fun!"

They giggled evilly and got back to work.

Later that night over dinner, they told Papa Joe about their encounter. Papa Joe got the same evil grin on his face and started laughing. "Do you remember that old comedy show where the guy pretended his legs were buried in the dirt? Dorf?"

Lauren nearly spit out the tea that she had just sipped and laughed out loud.

"That's it! Oh, shit, that will be perfect."

* * * * *

A few weeks later, by the end of the first week in March, Lauren had the scoop on Marilyn from the other neighbors and knew her morning walk routine.

Since St. Patrick's Day was coming up, Jimmy and Lauren decided to dress Papa Joe up in a Leprechaun outfit with his shoes where his legs ran out at the knee.

They waited until just before Marilyn's return trip to stage him near the mailbox.

Marilyn walked by and suddenly stopped. She did not remember that elf-like person there on her way out. Papa Joe was as still as could be until she reached out to touch him.

In his best Irish accent, he called out to her, "Top of the morning to you, Marilyn."

She squealed and jumped higher than you thought an old lady could.

"Oh, Jesus Christ! Oh, wait, how do you know my name?"

"Oh, Marilyn. I'm a leprechaun. I know everything about you. My clan has been watching you for years now." Papa Joe laid it on thicker and thicker as he went along.

Marilyn stiffened up a bit. "Well, how come I have never seen you? I make it my business to know everyone on this block."

In an exasperated voice, Papa Joe answered. "Jesus, Mary, and Joseph, woman! Don't you know anything about leprechauns? We only appear when we want you to see us. You should be a lot nicer and less nosy with your neighbors. They don't like you very much."

"What? I am not nosy. Who told you that?"

"Like I said, we have been watching you for years. You most definitely are nosy! Like three weeks ago, when you were looking through the Johnson's screen windows while they were on vacation. Remember that? We know you look through everyone's mailbox, too! That's a federal offense, you know. Or what about when you yelled at that delivery driver just because he was Black? Oh, for shame! And you call yourself a good Christian?" The elf waggled his bony finger at her and shook his head.

She scurried down the street and did not look back until she got to her house.

When she was out of sight, Jimmy ran out to scoop up Papa Joe and get back inside.

Lauren had been recording the whole scene with her phone. They howled with laughter and could not wait to share the video with the neighbors.

* * * * *

A week later, Papa Joe was settled in and getting used to having his own place, even if it was just a few steps away from the main house. Jimmy had put in an intercom between the two houses so they could keep in touch, just in case Papa Joe needed something.

That Saturday, he and Jimmy were having coffee on the porch while Lauren had gone into town to do some shopping and have a latte with her dad.

"Jimmy, I am kinda liking this arrangement we all have. It seems to be working for me. However, now that you have moved in with your woman in her house, I am wondering when you are going to ask her to marry you? I kinda would like to see you married off, before it's my time. That's certainly more sooner than later, I'm sure."

"You know, Dad, I have been wanting to talk to you about your final wishes."

"Ah, not right now. I don't even wanna think about it. Stop dodging the question!"

"Okay, but it can't be forever. I don't want to have to guess what you are thinking."

Although the question from Papa Joe came out of nowhere, it didn't surprise Jimmy as much as he thought it would.

It was a reasonable question and one that had been on Jimmy's mind for a while. There had been a few events that tested their relationship. They were still together and seemed stronger than before.

"You know, Dad, a few months ago, I would have told you that you were crazy for thinking I was going to propose any time soon." He took a long pull off his coffee and continued. "However, the last couple of weeks have really opened my eyes. I believe she is *the* woman for me and I shouldn't procrastinate any longer."

Papa Joe had a big smile on his face. "It's about time, son, I think she is just perfect for you and I'm kinda in love with her, too. You'd better not let this one get away."

"I don't have a ring yet, but I am going to ask her friend, Joni, to help me with that. As far as the asking part, I think I am going to use the treehouse."

"The treehouse? What treehouse?" Papa Joe queried.

"The custom treehouse I built a few months ago that she helped with. She hasn't seen the completed project, but she helped with some of the design and structural issues. I think it would make a perfect spot, Jimmy-style."

Papa Joe laughed. "You may be right, I never figured you to be the flowers and candy romance guy. This might be right up your alley. How are you gonna do it?

"I don't know yet, but I am thinking some sort of surprise might be in order."

"That sounds like fun. You know, you have to include me in the surprise. What can I do to help?"

"I don't know yet, but you will be part of this, for sure. I think it will take some organizing and doing stuff in secret. I can't wait. This will be fun. A little stressful, but fun."

* * * * *

A few days later, Jimmy was in the backyard of Mrs. Olson's house, about to start work on a new deck for her.

She lived on the outskirts of town at the base of the local mountain range.

One advantage to her location—that other than peace and quiet from the city noise—was the wide range of wildlife that she got to look at while having her coffee on the deck in the morning. Rabbits, quail, coyotes, and the neighborhood feral cats all came by for a visit. Even though she had fencing all around her yard, and didn't leave food out, they sometimes got through for a closer visit. Maybe they hoped to get lucky.

Jimmy's project was to clear out the old, wobbly, failing deck and replace it with a bigger and better one.

She also reported that she had heard some weird sounds coming from under the deck boards.

"I'm sure it's nothing to worry about, probably just some rabbits making noise. I'll be just fine," said Jimmy nonchalantly.

"Okay, Jimmy, if you say so, but it didn't sound like any rabbit I've ever heard."

Jimmy grabbed his tool belt, a screw gun, and a big shovel from his truck, then headed for the backyard. Most screws came out just fine except for a few that needed some persuasion from a hammer.

Bam! Bam! Bam!

His hammer struck the old wood.

Squeeee!

Jimmy jumped.

"What the hell was that?"

Nothing else came of it so he went back to work after taking a quick drink of his water.

Bam! Bam! Bam!

Squeeee, squeeee, squeeee!

The rustling under the deck board got louder. Jimmy backed away, dropped his screw gun, and grabbed his shovel, just in case. He got a whiff of an odd stink. He couldn't quite place it but it was strangely familiar to him.

Just as he finally recognized the smell, a giant javelina was staring at him from the end of the deck. Its hackles were raised.

The stinky, pig-like monsters are known for having poor eyesight.

It kept creeping closer to Jimmy. Jimmy inched backward.

Yelling and raising his hands to appear bigger than he was, Jimmy hoped that it would just run away. Instead, it rushed at Jimmy with surprising speed. He hit it with a glancing blow from the shovel.

Squealing from the impact, it spun around and sank its teeth into Jimmy's leg.

With blood gushing from his leg, he swung the shovel again.

Clang! Jimmy delivered a solid whack to the hard head of the giant animal. Mrs. Olson heard the ruckus and stuck her head out to see what the noise was about.

"Call 9-1-1!" Jimmy yelled at her.

The creature recovered from the second strike and was charging toward Jimmy once more. Another mighty swing and the shovel handle splintered upon impact. The beast clamped down on his leg one more time.

"Bloody hell, get off me!"

He took both of his gloved hands and grabbed it around the neck. With his adrenaline-fueled strength, he picked up the javelina and slammed it against a tree. It fell to the ground and lay still as Jimmy backed his way into the kitchen and shut the door.

He sat on the floor while Mrs. Olson wrapped towels around his leg to control the bleeding.

"The paramedics are on their way now," she reported as she looked out the window. "That thing isn't moving anymore. What was that?'

"That was a javelina. Normally, they are afraid of humans and will run away whenever they can. They are usually in packs, too, so I don't know where the rest of them are."

The paramedics arrived and got to work on Jimmy's leg. With the bleeding stopped and a shot given for the pain, they loaded him up in the ambulance.

Jimmy called Lauren from the back of the ambulance.

"Hi, sweetie. Can you meet me at the ER? I just had a fight with a javelina at Mrs. Olson's house. I'm in the back of the ambulance right now."

"Oh, my God, Jimmy. Are you okay?"

"Yeah, I'll be fine. I think he got it worse."

"Okay, I am on my way." She started laughing. "You aren't going to make this a habit now are you? This is twice now."

"Oh, ow! Don't make me laugh. It hurts. I hope not. Okay, I will see you soon. I love you."

A little while later, Lauren found her way to his hospital room.

"Oh, perfect timing. Dr. Parker just got here."

"Well, Jimmy," Dr. Parker said, "the game warden just called and verified that the javelina had rabies. That's why he kept coming after you rocked him a few times with the shovel. So, you will have to get the series of rabies shots. But he was dead upon arrival, so the tree did the trick."

"It all happened so fast. It's gonna leave a good scar, though. Chicks dig scars, right?"

He laughed as Lauren playfully punched his arm. "Ow! No more hurting the patient."

"After the first shot, we will monitor you for any adverse effects. If there are none, then Lauren can drive you home. You will need to stay off that leg for a few days to let the stitches do their job." With that, the doctor left the two alone.

"I've already called Cici and told her to head over to Mrs. Olson's house, to check in on her and lock up your stuff. Papa Joe knows, too."

Chapter 16: The Proposal

A few weeks later, in mid-April of 2015, after Jimmy had completed the remaining doses of the rabies vaccine and his injuries had fully healed, he and Lauren were in town, having breakfast at The Coffee Stand. They had taken separate vehicles because Lauren had an appointment with a client that morning and had made plans to get together with her father for lunch, a latte, and some "catch-up" time. Plus, Jimmy was scheduled to do a few jobs that day.

Jimmy normally had a full breakfast of eggs, bacon, toast, and hash browns. Today, however, he was having only toast and coffee.

"Aren't you hungry, Jimmy?" Lauren asked, noticing his smaller-than-normal breakfast. "What's wrong?"

"Ah, nothing wrong at all. I just didn't feel like eating a bunch today."

He hoped that he had convinced her that everything was okay. In fact, he was hoping everything would be more than okay—and maybe even life-changing—by the end of the day.

It was Friday, April 17th, 2015, and they had known each other for about a year. Everything had been going great, with the exception of that one fiery incident, which got resolved fairly quickly. Since they had been living together, things had gone exceptionally well. They had a lot in common and worked well on projects together, too. Jimmy knew in his heart that Lauren was "The One."

Lauren had been especially helpful in the beginning stages of the treehouse project. Her engineering and decorating experience had come in handy during the design stage. She had been out to the treehouse a few times, in the early stages of the build. Due to her busy schedule, she had not yet seen the completed project.

What Lauren didn't know was that he planned to propose to her that very evening at the treehouse.

"How do you feel about an early dinner, around five?" Jimmy asked, drinking the last of his coffee.

"Sure, that sounds great. It's been a crazy week and I don't feel like staying out all night." Lauren sounded a little more tired than usual.

"Great. I'll swing by to pick you up around four-thirty, after I'm done with my last job. Oh, yeah, bring your sneakers!" Jimmy said with a wry smile and a twinkly eye as he got up to leave.

"What? Why?"

"Just trust me. Now, I have to get rolling. I have a ton of work to do today before dinner." With that, he left the diner, jumped in his truck, and sped away in a cloud of dust.

Jimmy was always doing something to surprise Lauren. He loved to see the look on her face when she got surprised. It was one of the things that made him fall in love with her so quickly.

Lauren didn't initially put much thought into his instructions. She was used to him pulling little stunts and surprises.

As the day wore on, she began to think about things a little more. It was curious that Jimmy only had a light breakfast. Now, she was beginning to wonder what he was up to, and what she would need sneakers for.

A few days prior, Jimmy had talked to Lauren's girlfriend about what kind of ring she might like. Joni was only too happy to help out, as she loved both of them. She could not have been more excited.

They went to a neighboring city so Lauren wouldn't see them in town. Lauren was known to go shopping downtown near the jewelry shop just a few doors away.

Jimmy had also asked his clients with the treehouse if he could propose there. They were thrilled to be included on his special day and happy to help in any way they could. It was their job to quietly gather his friends and family and hide them in the barn, then once Jimmy and Lauren were in the treehouse, they would appear on the ground below it, waiting for the sign from Jimmy that she said yes.

Papa Joe was probably the most excited of everyone. He loved Lauren right from the first time they met and had a feeling this would happen. Patti—another close friend of Lauren's—was in on the plan. Her job was to steal Lauren away for a girl's afternoon at the spa and to have Lauren home in time for Jimmy to pick her up. Patti then picked up Papa Joe on the sly, after dropping Lauren off from their afternoon trip to the spa.

The treehouse itself was a work of art.

The owners had given him a list of must-haves and left the rest for him and Lauren to design. It was built 20 feet up, between a few trees. It had a grand, winding staircase around one of the trunks, which led up to a large, wooden deck with railings. Planters full of roses lined the deck.

The deck also contained a gas fireplace surrounded by comfy chairs just right for enjoying the peace and quiet on the ranch. The light inside the great room came through a wall of windows on both the east and west sides. The treehouse would be a wonderful place to catch the sunrises and sunsets that their part of the country was known for.

One of Jimmy's woodworking masterpieces in the house was a hidden bedroom and bathroom. If you knew just which book to pull on the shelf, you could open the secret door.

At 4:00 p.m., it was time to put his plan into action. Jimmy checked in with everyone. They were all in their places. The ring was tucked safely in the secret bedroom so that he wouldn't accidentally lose it. He was able to get cleaned up at the owner's place. He brought a change of clothes with him so he could do that.

Jimmy rolled up right one time. He walked inside while hiding a bunch of flowers behind his back. Lauren was waiting for him, sneakers on.

"Wow, Jimmy, you look so handsome! Where in the world did you change and get dressed up like that?" Lauren was puzzled but smiled. It was hard to hide her smile whenever she saw him.

"Why, thank you." He pulled the flowers from behind his back. "These are for you."

Her surprised look was soon followed by a frown.

"Uh-oh, what did you do now, Jimmy?" Lauren asked.

"Nothing. Really! I just saw these flowers and they were calling your name."

"Okay," Lauren said with a smile that let him off the hook. She put them in a vase of water and asked, "Where are we going? I don't think I am dressed up enough for this."

"Believe me, Lauren, you look wonderful. I can't tell you. It's a surprise. You will just have to trust me, but I am certain that you will love this place."

About halfway to the ranch, Jimmy told her that she would have to wear a blindfold for the last mile or so. It was all part of the surprise. Lauren was game for just about anything, which was another thing that he loved so much about her. She was always supportive of his dreams, too.

A popular song from the 1990s came on the radio. It happened to be one of Lauren's favorites. Jimmy sang along at the top of his voice, "We built this city, we built this city on... 'sausage rolls.'"

"Jimmy! What? That is not how that goes. 'We built this city on rock and roll' is the line!" She was laughing so hard at Jimmy that she didn't notice the truck slowing down.

He pulled over and handed her the blindfold. Once it was on, he checked to make sure she couldn't see. He knew she would try to peek just a little bit. She began asking lots of questions, trying to get him to spill the beans. Jimmy was smiling so hard and was happy that she couldn't see him.

"Jimmy, this is killing me! What's going on? If you tell me now, I will go topless for the rest of the trip!" Although he was tempted, he held fast and didn't take the bait.

"Oh, really? Hmm. Nope. While that is a good idea for later, this will be much better."

Before Jimmy finished the blindfolded part of the drive, he stopped to text Patti to tell her that they were around the corner and also to ask if everything was set up. The short pause added to Lauren's anxiousness. She had no idea what he was up to.

Patti had successfully gotten everyone hidden in the barn.

They had glasses and bottles of champagne ready to pop if Lauren said yes.

Jimmy rolled up to the base of the tree and went around to Lauren's side of the truck to help her out. He took her arm and guided her up the perfectly laid stone pathway.

"It's okay. I got you. Watch your step. You're doing great, just a little bit more. Okay, stop! What I am about to show you will change your life. Are you ready for this Lauren Perry?"

"Yes, yes, yes!" The excitement in her voice now could not be hidden.

"One, two, two-and-a-half—" He tried to stretch it out as much as he could. "Three!" He pulled off the blindfold with one quick movement and let it drop to the ground.

As Lauren took in her first look at the completed treehouse, she was speechless. A tear rolled down her face.

"Oh, my God, Jimmy, this is beautiful," she said, between sniffles. He handed her a tissue.

"There's more! Follow me upstairs."

The smell of the trees and fresh air filled her senses as they made their way up the grand staircase, up to the patio deck with chairs and roses everywhere. The scent of cut lumber always made her happy.

As Lauren looked around in earnest, she saw her designs and ideas in place. She let out an "Ooh" each time she discovered another beautiful detail.

She stopped when she got to the bookcase that covered a large section of the room. For some reason, it just seemed out of place. She furrowed her eyebrows curiously.

"There is another surprise for you." Jimmy smiled.

"What? I don't think I can take any more surprises. This is fabulous!"

"Reach in the bookcase and get me the copy of *Gone with the Wind*." Not only was it the owner's favorite book, it was also one of Lauren's.

She found it and tugged at it. As she pulled on it, she heard a series of clicks.

A worried look crossed her face and she stepped back a little bit. The bookcase slowly slid back into itself to reveal the hidden bedroom. She squealed with delight.

"What? No way, a hidden room! This is the coolest thing ever!"

She entered it, awestruck.

While she was looking around, Jimmy retrieved the ring from its hiding spot and slipped it into his pocket.

The sun was starting to set outside and had turned the sky a million colors of red and blue. She went to a window and took in the view. Then, she turned around to face Jimmy.

"You have outdone yourself! You should be very proud. I know that I am." She gave him a big kiss.

He took her hand and led her over to the handmade railing fashioned from branches. He faced her, then put his hands around her shoulders.

"Lauren, from the day I met you, I never stopped thinking about you, your laugh, your eyes… and how hard you hit me when I tell a bad joke."

She put her hand over her mouth and giggled.

He continued, "You have always been there when I've needed you, and that is priceless."

He got down on his knee and withdrew the little blue box from his pocket.

"You are the best thing that has ever happened to me and I want to make you as happy as you have made me. Lauren Perry, will you marry me?"

He looked up into her eyes. They filled with tears. She was speechless. She couldn't tell anyone, but she had been waiting for this moment from the first day she met him, too.

"Oh, yes! I would be happy to marry you!"

The ring slid onto her finger like it was made for her. He stood up and she kissed him for what seemed like forever.

Meanwhile, their friends and family had quietly gathered at the base of the tree, champagne glasses in hand. Just when Jimmy knew they were all there, he leaned over the railing as if he was talking to the trees and shouted, "She said yes!"

Lauren was taken aback one more time as champagne corks started popping and a cheer came up from the crowd below.

Lauren smiled at her friends and looked at Jimmy with a gleam in her eye as she playfully punched him in the arm one more time. Again, she was speechless and happy.

Papa Joe looked up at the two from his wheelchair and beamed.

* * * * *

Dear Mom,

She said yes! Can you believe it? She said yes! She wants to marry me. I think Dad is more excited about it than I am. He almost jumped out of his chair. I can feel you smiling

*on me—on us—right now, Mom. I wish you
could have been there.*

* * * * *

The next morning was Saturday and Papa Joe was feeling restless.

Papa Joe was still excited from the night before and wanted to get out of the house a little bit. Sometimes, it was a big hassle because of the wheelchair. He didn't like imposing on Jimmy any more than he had to.

"Hey, Jimmy?"

"Yeah, Dad?"

"Do you think we could go to the store today, that big one? I don't feel like sitting around today. I'm getting a little stir-crazy."

"Sure thing, Dad. When do you want to go?"

"About an hour or so."

"Yeah, I can make that happen."

When Jimmy and Papa Joe rolled into the store's parking lot, it seemed busier than usual. Parking spots were tough to find. Jimmy spied a handicapped spot up front and headed for it quickly. From the other direction, a young lady in a black convertible sports car whipped into the spot right in front of Jimmy.

Jimmy honked his horn at her as he rolled down his window.

"Hey, you can't park there. You don't have a tag and I do. You need to move your car right now, please."

The girl was dressed in workout gear and certainly showed no signs of physical impairment. She tossed her ponytail around and yelled back at him.

"Oh, shut up, and mind your own business!"

"Really, that's your response? Well, okay, but remember that karma sucks!"

Jimmy flashed an evil grin at her as he rolled up his window and drove around.

"What the hell was that all about?" Papa Joe asked. He was upset at the whole thing, too.

"Don't worry about it Dad, I got this. You just enjoy the show!"

Jimmy pulled out his phone. He had his repo friend, Alex, on speed dial.

"Hey, Jimmy, what's up?"

"I have a YouTube special for you. Ya want it?"

"Ooh, yeah, yeah, yeah. Where are you?" Jimmy told him. "Okay, I will take it from here. Enjoy the show!"

Within ten minutes, Alex's black repo truck came rolling through the parking lot. He spotted the offending sports car. It only took a few seconds to deploy the boom from its stealthy spot in the back of his truck and hook onto the car.

Papa Joe could not believe his eyes. "He's not gonna do what I think he is gonna do, is he?"

"Yep. He is. He hates handicap offenders almost as much as I do. So now, if he sees one, or if I call him, he will come do this to it. Then he films the whole reaction on his phone to post on his YouTube channel. "

Papa Joe whistled softly and started laughing. "I'm telling ya, God works in mysterious ways, doesn't He? I hope this chick learns her lesson. This is going to be fun."

As quickly as he rolled in, Alex rolled back out with the car in tow. On the other side of the parking lot, about 100 yards away, he dropped the car under a palm tree. After returning the boom to its hiding place, he parked next to Jimmy, who was just a row away from the action. He jumped in the seat behind Papa Joe.

"Papa Joe, it's nice to see you again. It's been a bit."

"Hey, Alex, it's great to see you again. This is going to be fun."

A few moments later, a real handicapped van took the spot that had just been vacated.

About ten minutes after those people went into the store, the young lady came be-bopping out with a tiny bag in her hand. She looked at the van in disbelief. It was right where she left her car. Confused, she looked back at the store and then back the van that was in her spot. It was obvious she was upset because the three guys could see her arms flustering about, but they were too far away to hear what she was actually saying. She thumbed a few times on her phone and was soon talking to someone.

Ten minutes later, a police car rolled into the parking lot. It was a slow day for the officer. Policemen didn't normally respond to stolen car calls.

Alex waved him over.

In his line of work, he knew most of the patrol officers in town. This one was one of his favorites: Officer West. He told the patrolman what had transpired. Officer West nodded his head, gave him a wink, and said, "I got this. This will be fun."

After a little bit of discussion with the distraught lady, Officer West summed it up for her.

"So, you are telling me that you parked illegally in a handicapped spot, where you know you aren't allowed to park, and now you are complaining that your car is missing? You called me out here for this? You are lucky that I have another call to get to or I would be writing you a ticket for illegal parking in a handicap zone. That's good for about four hundred dollars. But I don't think your car is stolen. You just can't remember where you really parked it. I am going to leave now. It's reasonable to assume that if you use your little clicker, you might remember where you actually left it. Goodbye, and I hope your day gets better."

The police officer left. The young lady stretched out her arm, wildly clicking her car fob, pointing it in all directions, holding it like it was a magic wand. Finally, she heard a faint beep-beep. Then she heard it again.

She shaded her eyes from the sun and spotted her car across the lot under the palm tree. She picked up her bag and hurried over to her long-lost car. In her haste to get there, she tripped on a parking block. Her stumble caused her bag to rip open and her two bottles of wine fell to the ground. The impact shattered the glass and wine spilled all over the parking lot.

She screamed, then jumped up and down, waving her hands in the air in frustration. When her fit was over, she hung her head and slowly walked the rest of the way to her car. She got in and sat with her head over the steering wheel, frustrated and crying. When she looked up, a big white blob appeared on the windshield from the circling birds above.

Papa Joe, Jimmy, and Alex just laughed. Alex caught the whole scene with his phone's camera, too.

After Alex left, Jimmy and Papa Joe went shopping, as planned.

Chapter 17: Papa Joe's Wheelchair

Next to the guest house was an easily accessible terrace, and Papa Joe had found a great spot on it where he and Jimmy could continue their after-dinner drink tradition.

A third hand-carved rocking chair magically showed up on the terrace with Lauren's name on it. Jimmy had bought it during his adventurous outing with Papa Joe. Jimmy loved surprising Lauren just to see her face.

He opened a bottle of Macallan 18 and poured the whiskey into three glasses.

Papa Joe looked over at Lauren.

"Sweetie, now that you are going to be part of the family, you should know a little more of our history. I am sure that you have been curious about how I ended up in the wheelchair."

"You know, Papa Joe, I have been curious, but I wanted to wait until you were ready to tell the story. I am sure it's going to be a good one." She raised her glass to him and smiled. "I am all ears."

"Back many years ago, I was a boatswain's mate on a U.S. Naval Ship for a few years. We were coming into port after about three hard months at sea. I was part of the crew that ran the mooring lines to secure the ship to the dock."

Papa Joe took a sip and continued. "Those lines were made of nylon, not like the hemp they used in the old days. Nylon was used because it didn't mildew and it could stretch a little bit. There was a new captain on board doing his first mooring. We had one line attached and he had stretched it too far. We were yelling at him to back up a little, but he didn't hear us in time. Then there was a loud CRACK! Now, imagine a two-inch-thick rubber band snapping. Before anyone could even jump, that line came snapping back at the speed of light and it whipped through my legs like they were butter.

"I landed on the deck just in time to see one of my legs fly over the side. A corpsman, who was nearby, jumped on me immediately. He ripped off his shirt and covered my two ends as best he could. I screamed and then must have passed out from the blood loss and the pain. Next thing I knew, I was in a hospital bed. That was a really rough time for me because I had planned to be in the Navy for a lot longer than that."

He paused and looked around the room.

"Emma was my nurse. I found out her name a week or so later. They had me on so many pain pills that I was out of it for about that long. She could not have had a prettier name. It matched her perfectly. She would sit with me and talk until she had to finish her rounds. There was a lot that she had to do for me, and I felt bad that I couldn't do that stuff for myself yet. That put 'the humble' in me quickly. She changed my dressings, emptied my pans, and even had to bathe me. She was so gracious and never made me feel undignified during the process." He took a deep breath and another long sip of the amber liquid.

"I should have been more embarrassed about it but something told me that I could trust her completely. So, I listened to the little voice and put all my faith and trust in her. I was in that hospital for almost three months, healing and doing therapy. The doctors decided that I could try to move around and figure things out, but they also told me I was going to be medically discharged from the Navy.

"I got a wheelchair and soon learned how to get around pretty well on it. The other people in the hospital learned to get out of my way as I sped down those hallways or did tricks in the middle of them. One of my buddies worked in the machine shop on the base and made me a set of wheelie bars for the back.

"Emma used to scold me in public for being such a menace but would smile and high five me behind closed doors. I could always make that lady laugh. She didn't judge me for my lack of legs. She already knew who I was as a person just from talking with me all those late nights. I knew I was in love even before they discharged me."

Lauren was glued to her seat, her eyes locked on Papa Joe. She had a little sniffle as a tear rolled down her cheek.

"Oh, Papa Joe, that was an amazing story. Even now, I can hear how much you loved each other in your voice. Sorry for the tears."

Papa Joe looked up at the stars and raised his glass to them.

"Emma, your son has found a good one here. I think you would have been best friends by now." He drained his glass, said good night, and rolled away to his side of the house.

It was just about dusk. Jimmy and Lauren saw a family of four going for a walk down the street—a set of parents, a little boy on a bike, and a baby in a stroller. It looked like they were having a nice outing as a family.

"Jimmy, do you ever think you might want one of those?" Lauren asked, pointing to the kids going by.

Not really seeing what she was pointing at, he replied, "Want one of what?"

She burst out laughing. "A kid, you silly goose. Maybe a little Jimmy?"

He laughed out loud for a moment and then put on a serious face, "No. I really don't want one. I am not interested in being anyone's dad. That's why the last girl I dated dumped me. She wanted to be a stay-at-home mom with five kids."

The smile came back to his face as he recalled the short relationship that ended as quickly as it began. "The sheer look of horror on my face when she dropped that one on me pretty much told her everything she needed to know. What about you?"

She took a long pull on her whiskey. "I am an only child. I never wanted a little brother or sister. So, the kid gene must not be in me either."

"Okay. Well, that's good, because there is something else I wanted to talk to you about and it's a little sensitive."

A look of concern crossed her face as she sat straight up in her chair. She took another drink from her glass and looked Jimmy right in the eye.

"Jimmy, what's wrong?"

Seeing her react that way, he was quick to put any fears to rest.

"Oh, babe, there is nothing wrong. I was just thinking about getting snipped so we won't have an accidental pregnancy."

"You want a vasectomy?"

"Yes, I do."

She leaned an arm on the side of her chair, rested her head in one hand, and looked upward as she thought about it. A couple of moments passed, then she turned her head to look at him.

"Yes, sweetie. I am on board with you doing that. It is a lot easier for you to get that done than it would be for me to 'get fixed.' Plus, if you did, I could stop taking 'the pill.'"

They were happy that they were both on the same page, and couldn't believe they waited so long before having such a serious conversation.

Lauren leaned forward, showing more cleavage, and batted her eyelashes at Jimmy.

"By the way, I'd love to help you with the aftercare," she said with a wink and a sly smile.

A huge grin crossed his face. "Oh, boy! I have the doctor on speed dial. One moment, please!"

"Oh, Jimmy, you are impossible!" Lauren exclaimed, laughing as she playfully punched him on the arm.

Chapter 18: The Wedding

After months of planning and making arrangements, Jimmy could not believe that their big day had already arrived.

Once they had set the date—Saturday, August 15th, 2015—on the calendar, life went into whirlwind mode.

The week before the wedding, Lauren's father called her.

"Hey, sweetie, can you come by the house? I have something that I want to give you before the wedding."

"Oh, sure. What is it?"

"It's a surprise! I can't tell you, but I think you will like it."

"D-a-a-a-d!" Lauren drew out his name, then relented. "Okay, I will be over this afternoon."

The gravel crunched under her tires as she drove up to her dad's house. That sound always made her feel like she was home.

She pushed open the large oak door and soon found her dad in his study.

Finn was coughing. His breathing was labored, too. Lauren didn't notice any of that when he called her.

"Hi, sweetie. Before you get too close, I have to warn you that I am really sick. That was not what I called you here for, but I'm not sure I'll be better in time for your wedding."

Lauren froze in the study doorway. A worried look came across her face.

"Oh, Dad, I am really sorry. I know we were both looking forward to you walking me down the aisle. I hope you are going to be okay! The timing really sucks, but we will adjust, as we always do."

"Well, anyway, I have something for you that I probably should have given to you a while ago. But with all the stuff going on, I just forgot where I put it until now."

"What is it?" Lauren was curious.

Finn pulled a white box from underneath the desk.

"I know you didn't know you mother very well before she passed, but I think she would have wanted you to have this."

Lauren's eyes got misty at the thought of her long-lost mother.

She approached the desk and took the box from her father and carefully opened it. Inside was a lacy white vintage wedding dress.

Her dad further explained, "This was hers when we got married. I am not sure why I saved it this long. Your mom was a tiny thing, so I don't think this will fit you. But it's yours. You can do whatever you like with it."

With tears running down her face, Lauren said, "Dad, it's beautiful!"

She pulled it out of the box and held it up in front of her, and added, "Oh, yeah, she was tiny, all right. I must have got my size from your side of the family." Lauren's tears turned to a smile. She gingerly folded the dress and put it back in the box.

"Dad, I love you. Thank you for this. It means a lot. Don't worry, I will find a way to work it in. We are still putting the final touches on my dress. Wait until Jimmy sees this. He's gonna love it!"

"Oh, sweetie, I may have an idea about how to get you down the aisle. It seems you have taken a fancy to

Papa Joe. I would be more than proud to have him walk you down the aisle in my place. I will call him and ask. And if I'm better by next week, then I will come, too, and we can both walk with you."

Lauren started crying again. "Oh, Dad! That would be wonderful! I think he would be proud to do it, too. I can't wait to tell Jimmy."

So, a phone call was made and it was all settled. Papa Joe was honored to be asked and readily agreed.

* * * * *

Jimmy and Lauren decided to get married outdoors, in their yard.

The day prior to the wedding, landscapers had been over for the final time to make sure the backyard looked wonderful.

There was a balloon arch at the front to let the guests know exactly which house they needed to be at. The caterers had backed up their truck to the backyard and were busy setting up tables, chairs, and cooking stations.

Lauren was busy making sure that everything was going to plan and on time. Jeans and boots on, hair up in a ponytail, and a clipboard in hand, she barked instructions left and right.

One of Papa Joe's former Navy buddies came over, too, to help prepare Papa Joe for the big day. He'd return the next day, to help Papa Joe get into his old Navy uniform. Since Papa Joe was going to help give the bride away, he wanted to do it right. Lauren's dad was feeling a bit better and would be there, too.

By the time 2:00 p.m. came around the next day, the backyard was perfect. A circle of chairs surrounded an arbor covered in flowers where the minister and happy couple would be.

A section of the yard had been transformed into an outdoor kitchen, complete with a beautiful buffet. The grill station was manned by a chef ready to put the perfect sear on their steaks.

The minister wore a blue satin robe with black trim that matched her dark hair.

When it was time to get started, the quartet started playing Randy Newman's song called "You've got a friend in me."

There was one couple still missing.

Finally, they arrived.

Even from the backyard, you could hear the distinct rumble of a Harley Davidson. Rolling slowly side by side, Calvin and Carrie came up the street in style in their matching bikes with sidecars. They rolled to a stop in front of the house as Calvin hit the train horn he had installed. Everyone jumped and started laughing. The couple came in and quickly took their seats.

Lauren, her father, and Papa Joe appeared from the side gate. She had chosen a white silk dress. It had a sweetheart neckline and came down just past her knees. At the bottom of the dress, she had a seamstress sew on a four-inch band from her mother's dress.

Not a girl for heels, she wore comfortable white Converse sneakers. Her red hair was down past her shoulders and appeared to be glowing in the sunshine.

Papa Joe was right beside her, in his uniform. He could not have been prouder than he was at this moment. He was tickled that his only son was finally getting married to a good woman. As they came to a stop at the top of the semi-circle of guests, Lauren bent down to kiss

Papa Joe on both cheeks before her father wheeled him to their spots in the semi-circle.

The minister welcomed everyone and began to speak about marriage. Jimmy and Lauren had decided to write their own vows.

Jimmy cleared his throat before he started.

"Lauren, I wasn't looking for love when I knocked on your door for the first time, when I came to fix your squeaky cabinets. I was trying hard to keep my cool and hope you didn't catch me staring. I knew I liked you. Papa Joe knew right away that I was already in love with you, well before I did. I didn't realize it until you stayed overnight on the night of my fall. Nobody asked, you just stepped right in and took care of things like a boss. I love that you balance me out and I can't wait to spend the rest of my life with you."

"Jimmy, I was instantly attracted to you when you showed up to fix my cabinets and I was thrilled when my bathroom flooded and I had a good reason to call you back over. I fell in love with you for so many reasons. No one makes me laugh like you do and it is so easy to be my quirky self around you. I am happy to say that I want to spend the rest of my days with you."

The minister took both of them by the hand after they exchanged rings.

"By the power vested in me by the State of Arizona, I hereby pronounce you man and wife. You may now—."

Jimmy didn't wait for the minister to finish and immediately pulled Lauren into a big hug and then dipped her like a Broadway dancer.

"—kiss the bride. Oh, I see you are already there! Easy tiger, you have all night for that!"

The minister concluded with a laugh and a knowing smile.

Cheers went up from the crowd as the popcorn flew.

The DJ broke in and invited everyone to the bar to get started on drinks while the bride and groom headed off to have some wedding pictures taken.

About halfway through the reception, a strange lady, dressed in overalls and boots, had come through side gate. She appeared in the yard, yelling at everyone about parking on the street in front of her house like it was illegal. She announced that she was going to call the police.

Calvin got up from his seat and walked toward the rude lady.

"You are disrupting a private ceremony and you need to leave. It is not against the law to park on the street, even in front of your house. Now, please leave, or the police that will be called will be for them to escort you off this property."

"I am not leaving until someone moves their car from in front of my house. If they don't move it, I will have it towed."

"Is the car blocking your driveway? Is it blocking a fire hydrant?"

"Well, no. But it's in front of my house and it's an ugly car. It's one of those military hummer types and I don't like looking at it."

Calvin calmly walked over to the garden hose on the side of the house.

He opened the valve and put the nozzle in his hand, with his finger on the trigger.

"Ma'am, I have asked you kindly to leave but it is apparent that you are trespassing and refusing to respect everyone here. Leave quietly right now, or I will soak you from head to toe."

He squeezed the trigger on the sprayer a few times away from her to make his point.

She didn't budge.

"I am not moving until that person moves that ugly car and you can't make me. I am on public property right now."

"Ma'am, you opened a closed gate and are in my friend's yard! This is NOT public property!"

Without any further warning, Calvin completely soaked her from head to toe. She backed up, sputtering as the water hit her face. She quickly turned around and left, mad as a wet hen

After she exited, Calvin calmly shut and locked the gate. The rest of the party had gathered in a bunch to watch the antics. They clapped and cheered.

Lauren walked up to Calvin and gave him a great big hug. "Holy shit. That was epic! I have wanted to shut her up since Jimmy and Papa Joe moved in here."

Calvin laughed. "No problem. Consider that my wedding gift to you," he joked.

About an hour later, a police officer knocked on the side gate and peeked over. Jimmy saw him and went over to talk to him.

"Oh, hey, Jimmy. What are you doing here? A lady said that you sprayed her with water from your hose for no reason. What's the real story on that?"

It turned out that Officer Rivers was one of Jimmy's clients. Jimmy had installed a new fence for him just about a year ago.

"Hey, Tom! It's funny to see you uniform. I wasn't expecting to see the law today—especially one of my customers. Today is my wedding day, and we are having a nice party back here. That lady came over and walked through a shut gate, then proceeded to yell at us about someone that she thought parked illegally. Turns out she just didn't like that Hummer parked in front of her house. It wasn't obstructing her driveway or a fire hydrant. We asked her many times to leave and warned her that she would be sprayed if she didn't. She didn't leave and got sprayed."

The officer was laughing hard enough that he had to hold his hand on his stomach. "Well, we have heard from that lady a number of times for stupid shit like this. I am glad someone finally fought back. I will go talk to her and tell her she was, indeed, trespassing and breaking the law. Congratulations on your wedding."

"I am sorry you had to come out here just for that stupid lady. Can we get you and your partner some food to go? There's a buffet. Want to fix yourself a plate. There's even prime rib, garlic mashed potatoes, and wedding cake."

"Oh, that would be awesome! It's almost time for our dinner break, too."

"Sweet. Follow me! You can help yourself."

* * * * *

Later that night, after everyone had left and the backyard had been cleaned up, Jimmy and Lauren sat out on the terrace in their pajamas with glasses of whiskey. It had been a helluva fun day with their closest friends.

"Jimmy, have you given any thought as to what you want to do for a honeymoon?"

He shook his head with a grimace. "Nope. We have been so busy getting everything else done, that it plain escaped me. I never really thought about it much. Then again, I never figured on getting married until now either. Whatever it is we do, I want it to be fun for both of us."

"I hadn't really thought of it much either for the same reasons. It's okay, we can put it off for a bit, until things settle down here. Not every couple heads out immediately for a honeymoon. One of my clients waited a whole year to go on theirs."

Jimmy stood up with a goofy grin on his face. "I know what we can do right now."

Lauren cocked her head to the side, wondering what was going to come out of his mouth next.

"What?"

"We could go to bed now and get started on our honeymoon! I am kinda wondering if married lips taste better than non-married lips."

"Well, I declare, Jimmy, how you talk!" Lauren retorted in her best southern accent. Jimmy reached down and took his new wife by the hand.

"Yep, I think it's time I find out."

Chapter 19: The Parting Glass

A few weeks after the wedding, it was early September of 2015, and Jimmy and Lauren's schedules returned to normal.

One evening, Jimmy and Papa Joe were sitting on the terrace having their regular after-dinner bourbon.

Lauren was in the kitchen cleaning up. She was going to go to bed early because her day had been a tough one with finicky clients.

Papa Joe leaned over a little and looked at Jimmy.

"Ya know, Jimmy, I have been feeling a little more tired than usual. I can't explain it, but it's a little weird. Don't say anything to Lauren. She worries too much about stuff already."

"No problem, Dad. I know what you mean about Lauren. Anyway, this may be a good time to talk about your final wishes. I have tried a few times but it was just bad timing. We have never really talked about what you want. It might seem a little grim, but it's still stuff we should discuss. I don't want to have to guess later on."

"I know, Jimmy, and I've taken care of some stuff already. It's all in a letter with my lawyer, Mr. Williams. His office is downtown. I'll spare you the details because you know I don't have much. There is a life insurance policy, but I have no idea what it's worth. Your mom started all that stuff so long ago. What I do want is to be cremated, and whatever organs they can use, have them donated."

Jimmy took a long pull on his bourbon.

A moment later, he spoke.

"That's easy enough to do. Do you want a wake or an end-of-life celebration, as they are calling it nowadays?"

"Hell, no, Jimmy," Papa Joe said with a laugh. "I don't want a big fuss made over me. Most of my friends have already passed and there is no one I want there other than the two of you."

"Okay, Dad. That was about as easy a chat as ever. I'm glad I know now."

Papa Joe gulped down his last swallow and released the brakes on his wheelchair.

"I am going to head for bed. I am getting pretty sleepy now. I will have coffee on before you get up."

"Okay. It's a nice night, so I'm gonna stay out here a little longer. Lauren is probably already dead asleep."

Once Papa Joe rolled away, it got really quiet out in the yard. The only thing making any noise was an owl in the tree giving an occasional hoot.

An odd chill ran up Jimmy's spine and goosebumps covered his arms.

A random thought entered his mind. He shook it off.

"Nah, no way," he mumbled aloud.

Jimmy finished his drink and carried both glasses inside. He did his normal end-of-night routine he called his "walkabout"—walking around the house to make sure that all windows, doors, and cars were secured—before turning in.

He crawled into bed and Lauren shifted a little.

"Honey, are you okay?" she asked sleepily.

"Yeah, I just have a funny feeling, I don't know why. It'll go away, once I get to sleep, I'm sure. I love you and will see you in the morning."

"I love you, too," she whispered and rolled over.

Jimmy curled up under the sheet and tried to sleep. As he closed his eyes, he had a vision of his mom standing before him with her arms wide open, as though waiting for a hug.

His eyes flew open.

He threw off his sheet and just stared at the ceiling. He couldn't shake the odd feeling that had come over him.

He got up and walked across the breezeway to the guest house.

Papa Joe never locked his door because the backyard was already secured. Plus, he wanted his place to be easily accessed in case of an emergency or in case he needed help.

Jimmy tiptoed through the living room to the bedroom to check on his dad. He was fine, snoring like a lion, as usual.

Feeling satisfied, Jimmy walked back to the kitchen. He was thirsty. No one was looking, so he chugged some milk straight from the jug. He went back to bed after doing his walkabout one more time.

Their normal wake-up time was 5:00 a.m.

By the time Jimmy padded into the kitchen, Papa Joe usually had the first pot of coffee on. When Jimmy woke up, Papa Joe wasn't there. Jimmy thought, *No biggie. He probably decided to sleep in a little bit.* He had been pretty tired last night.

Jimmy started the coffee himself.

Around 6:00 a.m. was when Lauren usually made her appearance.

"Hey, where's Papa Joe?"

"He was pretty tired last night, so maybe he decided to sleep in. I'll give him a few more minutes and then go check on him."

"Okay, I'll be out the door shortly. I have a full day in front of me." Lauren filled her travel mug with coffee and set it next to her portfolio briefcase near the door.

Jimmy finished his first cup and kissed his wife goodbye. He decided he'd waited long enough and headed over to check on his dad.

"Dad!" he yelled as he went through the front door. "Dad, are you awake? Coffee time!"

There was no answer, so he headed toward the bedroom. That same chill from last night ran down his spine.

Papa Joe was still under the covers with a peaceful look on his face, just like last night. Jimmy felt his face.

It was cold.

Immediately, he knew. Papa Joe had passed away in his sleep.

Jimmy sat on the edge of the bed and sent a text to Lauren.

'Dad passed away in his sleep last night.'

Lauren was at a red light when she got the text. She immediately turned around and raced home. She flew through the house and breezeway to Papa Joe's house. She found Jimmy sitting in the side chair just staring off into space.

He stood up when she walked in.

"Oh, Jimmy. I'm so sorry." Lauren went to comfort him.

There were tears in her eyes. No more words were spoken as they hugged each other tightly. Jimmy picked up his phone and dialed the non-emergency police number.

Within half an hour, both the paramedics and someone from the coroner's office knocked on the door.

They examined Papa Joe and made the call on the time of death.

Jimmy and Lauren returned to the kitchen and started another pot of coffee. Lauren took out her phone and busied herself with canceling that day's appointments. Jimmy handed the paramedic the envelope with a copy of Papa Joe's final instructions.

Oddly enough, the fact that Papa Joe died peacefully in his sleep sat well with Jimmy and he was not as sad as he thought he might be. He had lived a very good life and died with no regrets.

Jimmy headed to his office to find his journal.

Dear Mom,

The day that I have been dreading finally came around. Dad passed away last night in his sleep. But then, you probably knew that already. I had a weird feeling when I saw you in my dream last night that something was up. I thought the open arms were for me, but I guess they were really for Dad.

All in all, it was a nice way to go, with no drama. Just like how he would have liked it. I suppose I am not too shocked. He did it on his terms.

I am going to miss him terribly. He was my best friend, dad, and mentor. I know he liked having me around, too, and not just to push him around.

* * * * *

Two weeks later, the cremated remains and death certificate arrived by courier.

The next day, per Papa Joe's request, Jimmy and Lauren drove around to his favorite spots, including their favorite fishing hole, to sprinkle his ashes.

* * * * *

A few weeks later, in early October, Jimmy and Cici were working on a customer's bathroom remodel. His phone buzzed in his pocket. Jimmy looked at the number. It was from Mr. Williams.

He tapped Cici on the shoulder.

"This seems like it's a good time to take a break. I gotta see what this voicemail is all about."

"No worries, boss, I'll go get us some coffee and be right back."

Jimmy took a seat in his truck and pushed a few buttons on his phone.

"Hi Jimmy, this is Mr. Williams, your dad's lawyer. There's no cause for alarm if that's what you are thinking. I would, however, like for you to call me when you get a chance."

Jimmy found his number and thumbed the button to dial it.

"Hey, Jimmy, thanks for calling me back so soon. Listen, if you didn't know, your dad had a few life insurance policies that you and Lauren are named on, but I'd rather not get into the details on the phone. Could you meet me at my office this week sometime?"

"He had a few? Wow, that rascally old man." Jimmy smiled. It was just like his dad not to talk about money if he didn't have to. He quickly looked at the calendar he shared with Lauren. "Sure. We can make it over the day after tomorrow."

Later that day, over dinner, Jimmy brought it up.

"You are never going to guess who called me today."

Lauren said between a mouthful of salad, "Oh, yeah, who?"

"Mr. Williams, Dad's lawyer. He said we need to come to his office the day after tomorrow. Dad had some life insurance policies that he never really told me about. He wouldn't say what the value was."

"Aww. That sweet old man. Even after he's gone, he is still looking out for his son."

Jimmy had no idea how much was involved, so he didn't want to start dreaming about fancy cars and wild vacations.

That wasn't his style anyway.

* * * * *

A couple of days later, they walked into the lawyer's office and were greeted by his assistant.

"Mr. Williams will be right with you. He is just finishing up with another client. Can I get you some coffee or water?"

"Sure, I will take a water, please," said Lauren.

"Nothing for me, thanks," Jimmy said.

A few minutes later, the big office door opened.

"Hey, Jimmy and Lauren, it's so good to see you. Thanks for coming down so soon. I heard about the excitement at your wedding party. That was epic. I wish I had been there to see it." They all laughed at the thought of the crazy neighbor being soaked from head to toe for being rude that day. "Anyway, let's get down to the business at hand. Your dad wanted me to wait a couple of weeks to let you know about these. He had a life insurance policy through the Navy and one that he and Emma started on their own. Both of them combined total nearly a million dollars."

Their eyes flew open while their jaws dropped at the news. They were speechless for a few moments.

Jimmy was the first to speak.

"Holy crap! Really? I had no idea. He glazed over that when we were talking about his final wishes, but that was it. I guess he wanted it to be a surprise."

Lauren chimed in, "Surprise!" She had a big smile on her face and her hands opened wide.

That got a quick laugh from Jimmy and Mr. Williams, who continued, "He left a note for you, too. It reads—" Mr. Williams unfolded a sheet of paper and perched his glasses on the edge of his nose.

Out loud, the lawyer read, *"Hey, Jimmy and Lauren. Gotcha! One last surprise from the old man. I know you will do smart things with this money but you should also have some fun. You've earned it. Love Papa Joe."*

Jimmy looked at Lauren. A tear formed in his eye. She took his hand and held it.

"I'll have the money wired to your account by the end of the week. Thanks for coming by. I am going to miss your dad and his crazy navy stories."

The lawyer clapped Jimmy on the back, then the men shook hands. Lauren leaned in for a brief hug before they parted.

Not much was said on the drive home. They were still processing the news.

Out on the terrace with a glass of whiskey, Lauren asked, "Well, New Husband, what do you want to do about this? Any thoughts?"

"Well, New Wife, I am not exactly sure yet, but a few thoughts have come to mind. I'd like to buy a new truck for Cici. She's earned it. It'll be a company truck so she doesn't have to cover any of the expense."

Lauren smiled at that idea. "Oh, yeah, she would love that, and yes, she's earned it for sure."

"I think I would also like to start up a fund so I can fix things for those people that don't have the money to fix stuff but still need it done. Kinda like how that traffic judge on TV does. Then the rest, I have no idea. Maybe just sit on it for a bit. We don't really need it right now."

Lauren asked, "What about Calvin? Does he need another investor for his sidecar venture? I wouldn't mind giving him some startup funds."

"I am all for that, too," Jimmy agreed.

As they watched the sun sink behind the horizon, they poured out the third glass that had been sitting there in honor of Papa Joe and raised theirs in a toast.

"*Sláinte*. I could not have asked for a better dad, and I know you are gonna be watching out for us."

Chapter 20: The Cruise

After a few weeks of back-and-forth honeymoon ideas, Jimmy and Lauren finally decided on a cruise. Neither of them had been on one. Now, with the money from Papa Joe, they could certainly afford to go on a nice one.

They decided to spend their Christmas and New Year's holidays on a honeymoon vacation. Their destination was The Bahamas.

Sailing day came and they left their luggage on the dock, like everyone else did, and found their room.

It was really nice for how compact it was. However, they didn't plan on spending much time in there except for sleeping and showering.

Jimmy and Lauren changed and were soon back out on the deck.

The ship cast off with lots of cheering. Fireworks and confetti filled the sky as they left the port.

They wandered up to the bow of ship and found two lounge chairs close to the railing. Holding hands and not saying a word, they felt the breeze on their face as they watched the sun dip below the horizon.

Jimmy looked at his watch. "Okay, the romantic part is over with. Let's go eat!"

Lauren punched him on the shoulder. "Jimmy Harper, what is wrong with you?" She feigned annoyance but it was hard to hide her smile. "Real smooth with the romantic part, buddy." She couldn't hold a straight face any longer and burst out laughing.

"Oh, shit, you are right. I am starving, let's go!"

They checked their phones for their seating assignment. They would be seated with two other couples.

One couple was a hip couple from Los Angeles.

The other couple was the youngest one they had ever met. No more than 19 years old, the young man was fresh out of Marine boot camp. His trim physique and ultra-short haircut gave him away. His wife had just graduated from high school. They were from a small town in the south and they had never really seen anything as fancy as everything on that ship. They were on their honeymoon, too.

As expected, the food was amazing. The hungry Marine, much to the table's amusement but not surprise, ordered three times, and all three times, he cleaned his plate.

* * * * *

Jimmy couldn't help but be an early riser. He found the coffee bar and then a good spot on the deck to watch the sunrise. There were a few other early birds and they all chatted about this and that.

Lauren woke up two hours later and texted him to meet her for breakfast. They ran into the Marine couple again. Not surprisingly, the young guy already had a few empty plates in front of him.

Later, Jimmy and Lauren headed down to one of the two pools. Of course, Jimmy picked the one with the slide. Lauren found their poolside cabana while Jimmy headed straight for the slide.

On the other end of the pool was a group of ladies. They were all wearing bikinis and had tropical drinks on the deck next to them. Jimmy was about halfway across the pool when they called out to him.

"Hey, would you mind taking some pics for us?"

Of course, he couldn't turn them down.

After a brief conversation, he learned they were a group of teachers on their winter vacation.

He didn't remember his high school teachers looking like that.

It wasn't long before they were all joking around and even had Jimmy floating on his side being held up by the ladies.

One lady, Linda, who seemed to be the ringleader, asked, "Where's your wife?"

"Oh, she is over there in the cabana," he said, pointing. He waved to Lauren, who waved back.

"She won't be mad?" Linda looked a little worried.

"No, she knows we are just having fun."

"Okay. I don't want you to get in trouble so early in the cruise. Hey, we are going to the nightclub later on tonight and to a pineapple party after that. Y'all seem like fun. Do you want to come with us?"

Jimmy scrunched up his face a little bit. He had no idea what a pineapple party was.

Linda smiled at him. "You don't know what that is do you?"

"No, I'm sorry, I don't."

Linda lowered her voice a little and got closer to him. "Have you heard of swingers?"

His eyebrows raised as his eyes opened wider. "Um, yes, but I have never known any."

"I understand," Linda continued. "If that is something that offends you or totally have no interest in, I will say no more and be on my merry way."

DAVID LASTINGER

Jimmy had heard of swingers a few times and was curious about how that all worked. Jimmy's face turned a few shades of red as he blushed.

"No, you are okay. We are all adults, but we are here on our honeymoon. It sounds interesting, but the timing is all wrong."

With a big smile, Linda exclaimed, "Fantastic, and congratulations! Y'all go have a great time together, and maybe in the future you'll think about it."

Jimmy walked over to their cabana and poked his head in. "Hey, what's up?"

Lauren sat up with a concerned look on her face. His face was red, and it wasn't from the sunshine.

"What's on your mind Jimmy? You can always tell me."

He took a deep breath and started in. "One of the ladies in that group invited us to meet them at the night club tonight, and then asked if we might be interested in a pineapple party afterward."

"Really? She's a swinger? I heard of such parties when I was living in Seattle. I never knew anyone in the lifestyle, though. Anyway, she wanted us to go? What did you say?"

"I told her that we were here on our honeymoon and that the timing was all wrong."

Lauren laughed, "Oh, good answer, sweetie! Now, how about you swing your cute butt over here and we hang out for a while?"

"Sounds like a marvelous idea." Jimmy grinned as his cheeks returned to their regular color.

* * * * *

The next morning, before Lauren awoke, Jimmy took his coffee and leather journal to his favorite spot on the bow.

Dear Mom and Dad,

Y'all would love this view right now. The sun comes up with the ocean breeze in your face.

I can't believe that I have finally been able to fulfill all your wishes that you had for me. I have a successful little business and a wonderful wife. The old people in the neighborhood still talk about you and all the things you did for everyone. I hope that I can live up to that standard.

I miss you and love you both. Thank you for everything you've done for me.

Please continue to watch over me... and Lauren, too.

About the Author

David Lastinger was born in Texas and currently lives in Phoenix, Arizona, with his wife, three dogs, and a cat. He has lived there long enough to be considered a native. When he's not working or writing, you can find him on an outdoor adventure—typically cycling, hiking, camping, or kayaking. One of David's proudest accomplishments is that he and his best friend have completed the first 500 miles of the Pacific Crest Trail.

David has worked at various jobs throughout the years. He spent 20 years in the hotel business, 10 years as a self-employed auto detailer, 10 years in the mortgage business, and some time as a courier for a medical supply company. He is currently working as a courier for an Arizona-based title agency.

David has been writing as a hobby since his college days. Many of his stories come from those experiences and his chronicles of them. He is happy he saved those journals.

This is David's third book. What started as short story in his second book, *The Blow-Off Letter and Other Fabulous Tales*, has been expanded into this novel. His first book, *How to Do Things Your Phone Won't*, is a self-help guide for anyone that is just getting out on their own. All books are currently available on Amazon.